Five Years
Too Long

Five Years
Too Long

A Novel

B. D. SINCLAIR

Published by 22 Degrees Press

ISBN (Paperback): 979-8-218-81352-9

Cover design by Bria Ingram

Printed in the United States of America

To healing messy and
imperfect, but always possible.

Chapter 1
Stillness Between Us

"I can do this," Myra muttered to herself, tugging at her watchband as she approached the newly constructed home. It had been five years since she last saw her.

Luna.

The name still sat in her chest like it belonged there. Myra turned her attention toward her assistant, Erica.

Erica was walking through the open house, making sure everything was set up. Starting over with someone new always felt like a chore—a different rhythm, a different energy. Jordan had known her inside and out: sharp, intuitive, reliable to a fault. Erica was still learning the flow, and Myra was too preoccupied with the past to really teach it. Especially today.

"Is everything in order?" Myra asked.

The nervous young woman shifted her weight and smiled a little too brightly. "Yes, ma'am. Everything's almost ready. Just waiting on you for the final walkthrough. The staging crew really nailed it, I think. All the décor's in place."

Myra arched an eyebrow, deciding to see how Erica would handle a little pressure. "Relax. I can feel your nerves. I promise, I'm not as difficult as I look." She offered a reassuring smile, though it did not fully erase the tension in Erica's posture.

Erica fiddled with the hem of her blouse, her fingers restless as they brushed against the soft fabric while she tried to steady her breath. She was doing her best to maintain control, but her hands betrayed her. Despite the jitters, she was not going to let her shot slip away. This was her chance to prove herself. She was more than just another assistant.

Myra scanned the living room, glancing at the large windows. Sunlight filtered through, casting soft shadows on the polished hardwood floors. The faint scent of fresh paint and new leather mingled in the air. She could sense Erica's uncertainty without even looking at her.

"Hey, Erica?"

"Yes, ma'am?"

"Do you ever joke?" Myra's voice was light, teasing, and she could not help but smirk.

It was quiet for a moment before Erica let out a nervous laugh, one that broke the tension. Myra followed with a low chuckle of her own.

Myra walked off, shaking her head. "Looks like I found someone with a sense of humor," she said.

Erica, still catching her breath from her awkward laugh, smiled sheepishly. "Not sure if that's a compliment or a warning.

Myra's smile lingered as she straightened some furniture. Her fingers brushed the smooth edge of a glass coffee table, the cool surface grounding her in the moment, reminding her of the importance of this deal.

She adjusted a vase on the mantle. Everything was perfectly staged—everything except her. Once, she might have believed in what this house represented: a fresh start, something lasting.

But she had run from that once, from someone who could have planted something real.

Now she was shaped by the seasons in between. Guarded, sure, but still here. Still showing up. Still hoping that, just maybe, it was not too late to rebuild what she'd lost.

"Is she on her way?" Myra asked, her voice a bit more even now.

Erica glanced at her phone, checking the messages. "She's due here any minute."

Myra did not look at her assistant but offered a small, knowing smile. "She'll be here in twenty minutes. Don't worry, I know her type."

Erica tilted her head, confused. "What do you mean?"

Myra's gaze flicked to the door, her pulse quickening. She wanted to believe it was just business, but her body disagreed. She brushed the thought away quickly. No need to dig into all that, not now.

Her tone turned casual. "If she's supposed to be here now, she's always fashionably late. Call it a habit." She shrugged as if it was no big deal, but there was something in her voice that said otherwise.

"Ah." Erica nodded, looking back down at her phone. "So, she's a perfectionist."

Myra's lips quirked into a smile. "Perfectionist? I guess you could say that."

"Have you worked with her before?" Erica asked, still curious. Myra's smirk deepened. "Not professionally. But I know enough."

Erica's eyes widened. "She's that good, huh?"

Myra looked at her for a moment, her expression thoughtful. "She's been an inspiration to me, even before all of this." She paused, then added with a small laugh, "It's about time I met her professionally "Erica practically bounced on her toes. "I can't wait to see her in person. She's the makeup artist in Nashville. I've followed her for years."

Myra smiled knowingly. "You're not just hoping to impress her, are you?"

Erica flushed slightly. "Not just... but yes. This could be my big break."

Myra gave a small, almost encouraging nod. "Good. Go on, then.

Show her in. I'm sure she's anxious to see the house."

As Erica rushed out to meet Luna, Myra took a deep breath, trying to center herself. The air around her felt thick, like a storm was about to break. The silence in the room only seemed to make it worse.

Luna pulled up to the house, her mind a whirlwind. It had been five long years since she last saw Myra, and this meeting felt strange. The past had a way of lingering in the back of her mind, unresolved and a little painful. Her hands tightened on the steering wheel, knuckles pressing against the leather as though her grip could keep her grounded in the present.

With a steadying breath, she released the wheel and opened the car door. Her heels clicked softly against the pavement as she walked toward the house, each step pulling her deeper into memories she was not sure she was ready to face.

Erica greeted her at the door with a warm smile, stepping aside to let her in.

"Hi, Luna," she said, holding the door open. "Come on in, Myra's just finishing up in the back."

Luna's heart was racing as she stepped into the house. The grandeur of the space almost felt overwhelming: soaring ceilings, walls bathed in soft ambient light, and sleek modern furniture. It was beautiful, no doubt. But it did not compare to the whirlwind inside her mind as she tried to take in her surroundings.

"Focus, Luna," she told herself, mentally shaking off the flood of memories that hit her the moment she crossed the threshold.

"This is business. You are here to do a job."

But her gaze kept drifting back to the woman standing near the stairs. Myra.

She looked just as she remembered, and yet not. The five years that had passed between them seemed to melt away in a single moment, only to be replaced by a rush of emotions Luna did not know how to contain.

"Why does it still feel like this? Like nothing has changed?" Luna wondered, her breath catching as her heart thudded loudly in her chest.

Myra was walking toward her with that confident, purposeful stride of hers. It had always been one of the things Luna admired, how effortless it looked.

Luna tried to turn her attention back to the house, to the tour Erica was giving her, but the walls felt too tight and her skin too hot, as if all the years apart were finally catching up to her.

Then Myra's voice broke through her thoughts.

"Luna."

The sound of her name was soft, warm, and inviting.

Luna turned toward her. Hearing her name had sent a shiver through her body. It was ridiculous how easily Myra could still rattle her, even after all this time.

What am I doing? Why is my body reacting like this? Luna thought, her pulse quickening.

She folded her arms tightly across her chest, a small act of defense. Wanting to lean in but needing to stay composed. This was not the time for softness.

But when their eyes met, there was no hesitation, no awkwardness between them. Instead, it felt as if time had slipped away entirely.

Myra stood there, looking at her with an intensity Luna had not expected. The look was not cold or distant. It was something different. Something familiar, like they were picking up a conversation that had been paused for far too long.

They embraced briefly. A simple gesture, but Luna felt the weight of it. The touch was fleeting, yet it was enough to make her stomach flip, enough to remind her of all the things left unsaid.

"Five years," Myra said, trying to swallow the lump in her throat.

"Five years and nothing has changed. Except... everything," she thought.

Myra stepped back slightly, her eyes scanning Luna's face as though searching for something there. She looked for signs of change, of distance, anything that would justify the silence between them. But all she saw was the same pull she had tried to forget, and the guilt that came with, wanting to feel it again.

The silence stretched, and Luna could feel the tension building. It was not just the years apart, it was something deeper, something unspoken between them. The weight of their shared past—the late-night talks, the stolen moments of tenderness neither of them ever acknowledged—pressed in around her.

Luna exhaled slowly, trying to steady herself.

Her voice came out softer than she meant it to. "Yeah. A lot can change in that time."

It was the safest thing she could say. Safer than asking why Myra never called, or why she still looked at her like that.

Myra nodded, the corner of her mouth lifting in a faint smile, but there was something behind it, something almost bittersweet. "Congratulations," she said, her tone shifting to professional. "I've seen your work. You've done well for yourself."

Luna met her gaze, fighting to keep her composure. Her heart still fluttered in her chest, but she forced her voice to remain steady.

"I could say the same for you. Who would have thought you'd become the top realtor in Nashville?"

Myra chuckled, shaking her head in the way Luna knew so well.

"I never thought I'd get here either. But here we are."

The words hung between them, but there was no further explanation, no discussion of the years they had lost. Neither of them seemed willing to address the elephant in the room—the silence that had stretched between them for half a decade.

And yet, here they were, standing in the same space, feeling the same magnetic pull, as if the distance had never really mattered.

Luna wanted to say something, but the question caught in her throat. *Maybe it doesn't matter anymore, she told herself. We've both moved on. But has she really moved on from me?*

Myra had always known her better than anyone—the woman who had been her best friend, the one person Luna thought she could tell anything to Myra's voice broke the silence, her tone casual again as she moved toward the staircase. "Ready to see the first floor of the house?" she asked. Her voice was smooth, but Luna could hear the faintest tremor beneath it. "I think you'll like it."

Luna nodded, forcing herself to focus. *This is business. Focus on the work. Do not let the past drag you in.*

But as they moved through the house, Luna felt the weight of the energy between her and Myra in every room and, every hallway. Every time she looked at Myra, that old ache resurfaced.

Myra turned to her, hesitating before responding. "What did you say?" Luna asked.

Myra smirked, catching the distraction in Luna's eyes. She wanted to ask what was going on in her head, but instead, she just repeated herself. "Are you ready to see the main suite?"

As she approached, she brushed her arm lightly against Luna's.

"Lead the way," Luna said with a sly grin, trying to hide her growing unease.

"Of course." Myra's voice was smooth again, though Luna caught the faintest tremor beneath it.

The main suite was grand, as expected. The windows opened to a sweeping view of the city, the reflective lights twinkling in the sun far below.

The room was everything Luna had imagined and more. The two double doors opened to reveal a massive space that felt almost regal, the kind of room where a queen might wake. The suite was large enough for a lounging area and a California king bed, with room to spare. Luna's eyes landed on the electric fireplace along the wall, and she pictured an 85-inch TV mounted above it.

Myra's voice pulled her back. "You're in love with it, aren't you?"

Luna felt the heat rising in her cheeks as Myra pointed out the features of the room. Myra raised an eyebrow, a playful glint in her eye that made Luna's heart skip a beat.

"Sexy?" she teased, her voice low, drawing out the word.

Luna struggled to keep her composure.

She had promised herself she would not let the past dictate this meeting. But one look at Myra, and all her carefully rehearsed indifference began to crack.

There was a part of her that wanted to reach out, to close the gap between them, but the years stood like an impenetrable wall. As they moved through the house, Luna was not sure if Myra still saw her as the same person she had once shared everything with, or if this was just… professional.

But when their eyes met again, something flickered in Myra's gaze. A quiet understanding. And for just a moment, it felt like they had not really lost all that time after all.

Luna smiled, a little distracted but unable to hide it. "I guess you could say that."

Myra's gaze softened, her tone becoming almost tender as she leaned closer. "You would look amazing waking up in the morning, sunlight beaming through those windows, reflecting off your golden skin."

Luna's breath caught at the unexpected warmth in Myra's voice. She turned to face her fully, raising an eyebrow. "Are you flirting with me? Myra blinked, a slight nervousness creeping into her expression. "Was it that obvious?" she asked, laughing lightly, though there was an edge of uncertainty in her voice. "I'm just painting a picture for you. You belong in this house."

Luna could not help but smile, her eyes narrowing slightly as she studied Myra. "I'm kind of flattered that I know you well enough to read that look in your eye," she teased, her voice soft but knowing.

Myra blushed, turning her head away to hide it as she ran her fingers nervously through her hair. She quickly moved toward the main bathroom, avoiding eye contact.

"You haven't seen the best part of your bedroom yet," she said, steering the conversation to safer ground. Luna took a deep breath before following her.

The bathroom was as grand as the rest of the room, but what caught Luna's attention immediately was the enormous shower with double entrances. As she walked toward it, a memory surfaced—a dream of her and someone, their bodies pressed together against a steamy glass shower. She shook the thought away, trying to focus.

Myra's voice broke through her thoughts. "I worry about you," she said gently. "Where did your mind just go?"

Luna blinked, unsure how to respond. "If you don't mind," she said softly, her gaze dropping to the floor, "I'd rather not say."

Myra paused, sensing the shift in the air. She nodded quietly, and they both stood in silence for a moment, each lost in the weight of their unspoken history. The years between them seemed to stretch and contract like elastic. Myra cleared her throat, trying to bring the conversation back to neutral ground. "Well," she said after a moment, "this bathroom is clearly designed to make anyone feel sexy. I think we can agree on that."

Luna chuckled, her voice low and flirtatious. "I suppose I can't argue with that," she said, hopping onto the edge of the marble sink, her eyes never leaving Myra's.

Myra smiled and held out her hand. "Come down from there. We still have more house to see."

Luna followed her lead, their footsteps echoing softly as they made their way back downstairs.

Meanwhile, Erica was busy directing the contractor through the changes Myra had suggested, pointing toward the far wall with a clipboard in hand.

"Hey, Erica?" Myra called out as they reached the bottom of the stairs. "Can you go to the car and grab my tablet? I have some things I want to show Luna about the house, some designs I think will really elevate the space."

Erica scrambled to do as asked, moving quickly toward the front door.

Myra watched her go, then let out a soft sigh. "She's learning. Still a little unsure of herself, but she means well."

"She's eager," Luna said, her gaze following Erica for a beat too long. "It's a good quality to have in an assistant," she added casually.

Myra turned to her with a small, knowing smile. "Yes, but she's too hesitant. I need someone who can follow instructions but also challenge me when it counts."

Luna raised an eyebrow. "I seem to remember someone who used to be just like that."

Myra chuckled softly, her gaze dropping. "Yeah, well, people change."

Luna couldn't help but press. "I've heard you've gone through quite a few assistants recently."

Myra's eyes flickered with something unreadable before she shrugged. "I'm not picky, I just know what I need. I need someone who can keep up, follow my instructions, but still be confident enough to question me sometimes. That takes guts."

Luna nodded, thinking for a moment. "How long have you been looking for someone?"

Myra hesitated, then met Luna's eyes, her voice quieter. "I had one… she was perfect in some ways. She knew exactly what I needed. But she's gone now. Been looking for about eight months to replace her."

Jordan had been more than just an assistant, she had been Myra's partner, too. But that part of the story was not something she was ready to unpack. Not yet.

Luna narrowed her eyes slightly. "So why isn't she here anymore?"

Myra glanced away, her gaze darkening. "She was the perfect assistant, but not the perfect girlfriend."

She caught herself wondering, just briefly, if she would make the same choices now—if she'd run again, or if she would finally stay long enough to see something grow.

Luna's jaw dropped at the unexpected revelation. "Wait, you and your assistant…?"

Myra's face softened with a faint smile. "Yeah. Life turned out differently than I expected."

Luna's mind raced, but she couldn't find the words. Her curiosity was restless, but she didn't want to push.

Myra, sensing the change in the air, gently moved the conversation forward. "Anyway, let's talk business for now," she said, pulling the tablet from Erica's hands as she returned. "I've made some changes to the design that I think will really make the house stand out."

Erica gave them both a polite nod. "Let me know if you need anything else," she said before quietly stepping out to give them space.

Luna nodded, but her thoughts were still racing. *So, Myra's dating history includes her assistant. Interesting.*

They picked up the tour again, but the air between them felt heavier now. Luna tried to focus, yet her mind kept circling back to the things Myra had not said about her past. Myra continued to explain the changes she had made, her voice confident and authoritative, though there was still a softness beneath it.

"Still processing?" Myra asked, watching Luna closely.

Luna nodded, her expression thoughtful. "It looks amazing. You really have an eye for interior design."

Myra gave a modest smile. "Actually, Erica made most of the suggestions."

There was a pause—a brief stretch of silence where neither of them quite knew what to say next. Something about standing in this space Myra had shaped, touched by both growth and history, made the moment feel heavier than it should have been.

Luna smiled, trying to lighten the mood. "Want to move in with me?"

Myra laughed lightly, the tension momentarily easing. "You're funny," she replied, but her eyes lingered on Luna a moment longer than necessary. "Well, how did it start?" Luna asked before she could stop herself. "You and your assistant?"

Myra's eyes softened as she leaned against the kitchen counter. "I met her while showing her family their dream home. A few weeks later, she started working for me. It all felt so professional at first—late nights going over staging options, long days setting up listings. But then one evening, while we were making last-minute tweaks before a big open house, she leaned over and kissed me. I wasn't expecting it. But there was something in that kiss, something I hadn't felt in years.

Luna's brows knit together as she let out a surprised little laugh. "So she just made the first move out of the blue?"

Myra chuckled. "Yeah, it was pretty sudden. But sometimes, that's how life works."

The conversation drifted to safer ground, but something in Myra's tone—or maybe what she didn't say—kept tugging at Luna.

What really happened between Myra and her assistant? And why was she so closed off about it?

Myra locked up behind them and walked toward her car. "I was going to stop by the office before heading home," she said over her shoulder. "You're welcome to swing by too, if you've got a few minutes."

There was a pause, an unspoken understanding hanging in the air before Luna finally nodded.

CHAPTER 2
TANGLED CONVERSATIONS

The sun had started to dip lower in the sky as they drove in separate cars.

Fifteen minutes later, Luna pulled into the small private lot outside Myra's office. The building was quiet, tucked between a bakery and a boutique, its glass windows reflecting the soft amber light of early evening.

Myra was already at the door, unlocking it, her silhouette framed by the fading light. Luna followed her inside, the click of the door behind them sealing off the rest of the world.

They didn't say much as they made their way through the office. Maybe they were both still processing. Luna wasn't sure. But as Myra opened the mini fridge and reached for wine, she felt something shift in the silence between them, something that hadn't been there before.

"Would you like a glass of wine?" Myra asked, her tone casual but her eyes never leaving Luna's.

"Sure," Luna replied with a small smile, the quiet tension still hanging between them.

Myra poured the wine carefully before sitting beside Luna on the couch, handing her a glass. The air between them was charged, the familiarity of their past intertwined with the budding attraction that lingered in the present.

Luna took a sip, her eyes flicking to Myra's as she adjusted her position, trying to ignore the flutter in her chest. "So, how did you get into real estate?" she asked, genuinely curious, eager to shift the conversation to something light. She needed to calm her racing thoughts.

Myra leaned back slightly, swirling her glass in her hand. "Well, I had been working in property management, and I fell in love with showings. I just fell head over heels for being in the field, especially with new construction properties. It's hard to explain, but there's this rush I get, and I'm completely addicted to it."

"Try me," Luna urged, intrigued by what could capture her long- lost friend's heart the way makeup had captured hers. Myra's passion for real estate was something new, something Luna hadn't seen before. She wanted to understand it.

Myra smiled, her expression softening as she took a deep breath, clearly savoring the memory. "Well, there's this feeling I get that just takes my breath away." She paused for a moment, collecting her thoughts before continuing. "I remember the first time I was in the field. I was driving up to a neighborhood that was being developed. It was a summer day, clear skies, the sun shining down. There were maybe twelve houses in this cove, all mansion-like, each one more impressive than the last."

Luna listened intently, her gaze never leaving Myra, captivated by the way she spoke, the way she seemed to relive that moment in time.

"It was a beautiful day," Myra continued, a soft laugh escaping her lips. "I know you probably think I'm weird, but the smell of new construction in the air just put this huge smile on my face. It was like I was smelling possibility, the future. You know?"

Luna's lips curved into a smile, her heart beating faster than it should have. "I get it," she said softly, her voice barely above a whisper. She could see the scene in her mind: a hot summer day, the scent of freshly built homes, the promise of something new—just like the way Myra was speaking now.

Myra's eyes darkened with a deeper passion as she leaned forward, her voice dropping slightly. "It was such a beautiful scene, and I couldn't help but think, I want to always be surrounded by real estate. It's everything I could have ever imagined it would be. I was high off satisfaction, you know? The kind of feeling you get when everything just clicks."

Luna nodded, feeling the intensity of Myra's words wrap around her. "I know exactly what you mean," she replied, her voice soft but filled with understanding.

Myra's voice softened even more, almost reverent. "Oh, and that feeling of walking through the doors of a freshly built house... seeing its beauty, knowing you're one of the first people to step foot inside. It's like the house isn't just a structure. It's alive, it's something special. I never wanted to stop feeling that."

She lowered her glass carefully on the table in front of them, her eyes locking with Luna's warm caramel gaze. The room seemed to grow quieter, the air thick with an unspoken connection. She paused, as if allowing her words to settle before continuing.

"There are no words to describe the perfection of it," Myra said, her voice hushed, her eyes filled with something Luna couldn't quite place. "A brand-new house—it's perfect without needing anything else. It just... is."

Luna's breath caught in her throat. The depth in Myra's voice was unlike anything she had heard before. She was so wrapped up in the passion that Myra spoke with that she didn't even realize how fast she was breathing until she tried to steady herself.

Myra moved just a little closer, her presence suddenly more overwhelming, and for the briefest moment, the world outside the office seemed to disappear.

"I just really love real estate," Myra said, her tone proud but almost vulnerable, as though she were sharing a part of herself she rarely spoke about. She gave a small, contented sigh, as if the words had finally freed something inside of her.

Luna swallowed hard, her pulse quickening as Myra's words settled deep within her. "I can tell," she murmured, her gaze still locked on Myra's, unable to look away.

The feeling between them was unmistakable now, the distance closing in a way neither of them seemed to want to stop.

"Are you dating anyone?" Luna asked, her voice a mix of curiosity and care.

Myra gasped at the unexpected question, her eyes widening slightly.

"I'm only asking because you mentioned your ex left a few months ago, and you didn't say there was someone else in the picture." Luna's tone was casual, but there was an underlying warmth, a genuine interest in Myra's life.

Myra hesitated before answering. "I'm not seeing anyone at the moment." She paused, her lips curling slightly. "To be honest, I'm not sure I'm ready for anything like that."

Luna nodded, sensing there was more to the story. "Are you?" Myra's voice softened, the question hanging between them, reflective.

Luna smiled, the corners of her mouth lifting gently. "No. My last relationship made me want time to myself." She took a slow breath, the words slipping out as if she had been holding them in for far too long.

"Time to yourself, huh?" Myra mused, her tone light but thoughtful, as if trying to digest what Luna had said. She shifted in her seat, crossing her arms lightly. "I get that. Sometimes, space helps more than anything."

Luna's gaze softened, her eyes searching Myra's face for any sign of understanding. "I just think relationships should be with someone who is on the same page as you. When that person doesn't really know what they want, or can't see a future with you, then what's the point of the relationship continuing?"

Myra nodded slowly, her expression thoughtful. "That I can understand," she replied, her voice quieter now, as though reflecting on her own experiences.

"So, what about your ex? What's it like dating your assistant?" Luna asked, the question slipping out more naturally than she had anticipated.

Myra's lips twitched, the faintest hint of amusement crossing her features before she replied, "Jordan was very sure of what she wanted. Just like how she knew I liked her but never acted on it, so she took it upon herself to pursue me. It was like she knew how everything was going to unfold, as if she could read my every move."

Myra looked down for a moment, her gaze flickering with something Luna couldn't quite place. "I, unfortunately, couldn't keep up with her. She was... wild, I should say. We ended because she felt I should have dealt with my past. She lost patience with me. I was taking too long to accept what I needed to from it."

Luna felt a wave of anger at the thought. "Did she not understand how you process your emotions?" she asked, her voice rising slightly, a hint of frustration sneaking in.

Myra looked up sharply, her eyes meeting Luna's. "Somewhat. But there's more to her reason for leaving, and that is a story for another time." Her tone became lighter, almost dismissive, as she downed the rest of her wine.

Luna raised an eyebrow, her gaze lingering on Myra. "You're not fooling me, Myra," she said softly, her voice laced with quiet insistence. "I know you too well. You're avoiding something, and I can see it in your eyes." Myra winced, looking away briefly, as though Luna's words struck too close to a raw nerve. "Don't give me that look," she said, her voice defensive but soft. "I just... I'd rather not dive into it right now. It's not something I want to talk about."

Luna smiled lightly, her expression softening. "Well, you know I'll always be the person whose arms you love to be in when you cry," she said, her tone teasing but threaded with undeniable sincerity.

Myra smirked, a playful gleam in her eyes, but the moment between them carried a quiet intensity that was hard to ignore. Their eyes locked again, and for a moment, neither of them spoke.

The tension broke when Myra's phone rang, its sharp tone cutting through the stillness. She glanced down, irritation flashing across her face. "I need to take this. I'll be right back," she said, standing with a quick glance at Luna.

Luna watched her go, a strange mix of jealousy and disappointment swirling in her chest. She didn't want to care, but she did. And the way Myra left so quickly, without a word or glance, made her feel like the past was already repeating itself.

She leaned toward the open door, straining to catch Myra's voice.

Whoever was on the other end, Myra wasn't happy about it.

"Yeah. Okay... and... No, Jordan, I... will, but not this second. Give me some time, okay? Thank you. I will. You know I will, but I'm working!" Myra's frustration bled through every word, her tone firm but weighted with exhaustion.

"I need to get back to work. Bye." She ended the call abruptly, her voice still edged with irritation.

Luna quickly moved back to the couch as Myra entered the room. She straightened her posture, as if pretending she hadn't been eavesdropping.

"Everything okay?" Luna asked, trying to mask the curiosity in her voice. "Do you need to leave?"

"No," Myra replied, her tone cool but not entirely convincing. "Just someone who needs something I can take care of later." She smiled lightly, steering the conversation back. "So, back to you."

"So, when did you move to Nashville?" Myra asked, her tone shifting with curiosity. "Last I heard, you were in Houston, working under Kerry Washington and her network. How was that?"

"It was a great experience," Luna said, her smile softening. "It gave me the clientele I needed to be known all over the United States. Honestly, When I moved last fall, I didn't think it'd be difficult. I'd just update my location, and boom—clients found me."."

"Damn, seems like working for her served you well." Myra smirked, clearly impressed. "I have to say, I'm impressed."

Luna chuckled, shaking her head. "It was a lot of hard work, but yeah, it paid off." She paused before continuing, "Do you plan on...?"

Her voice trailed off as the sound of footsteps approached the door. Her eyes darted to Myra, whose expression shifted into irritation, as if she already knew who was coming.

"What the hell?" Myra whispered under her breath, just as a light- skinned, petite woman appeared at the door Luna's gaze froze. The woman was beautiful—small, but with curves in all the right places. Her full lips and big, captivating eyes caught Luna's attention, and the braids in her hair made her look like a scene straight out of Poetic Justice.

But it wasn't just her beauty that caught Luna off guard. It was the seductive smirk that played on the woman's lips, slowly melting into a knowing smile.

"What are you doing here?" Myra's voice was sharp with irritation.

Luna's eyes widened at the name she hadn't expected to hear today. Jordan.

"I just thought I'd drop by to use your letterhead to write the recommendation I needed myself," Jordan said, her tone dismissive.

Luna tried to hide her surprise. *This is Jordan?* she thought, forcing her composure. *Hmm, okay.* Her brow furrowed slightly.

Myra sighed. "I'm working right now. I don't have time to write the letter."

Jordan didn't seem bothered. "That's fine. That's why I can write it, and you can sign it. I know you like the back of my hand anyway."

Her gaze shifted to Luna, tilting her head slightly as if sizing her up. "I'm Jordan. Myra's rude and doesn't know how to properly introduce people. You must be Luna."

Her tone was respectful, but Luna caught the underlying challenge. "Hi. And yes, I know who you are," Luna replied, her voice smooth and confident, though her eyes carried a glint of something else.

"Myra's told me about you before," Jordan continued, her voice laced with mischief as she shot Luna a sly look. Luna couldn't help but laugh softly. "She's told me a lot about you, too."

Their eyes locked, the tension between them palpable. Both had made their claim.

"Well, you guys can go back to doing whatever you were doing," Jordan said, her words sharp but playful as she casually twirled a lock of Myra's hair before exiting the room.

"I'll be right back," Myra excused herself, following Jordan out of the office.

Luna watched as Myra left, then edged closer to the open door, trying to eavesdrop on their conversation.

"Baby, I'm sorry. I just needed the letter a little sooner than you could do it for me, so I thought it would be easier if I just came up here and did it myself. I won't be long, I promise. You can sign it, and then I'll be out of your hair."

"First off, I'm not your baby," Myra snapped, her voice laced with irritation.

Jordan smiled seductively, stepping closer. She placed her hands on Myra's hips, her touch lingering. "Look, you still mean a lot to me, and I was really insensitive when I walked out on you."

Myra didn't pull away, but she didn't lean into the touch either. Her body was rigid, her posture defensive. "And you choose this exact moment to tell me that? Why?"

"Did you know Luna was going to be in town?" Myra's voice dropped to a softer, almost casual tone. "Have you been keeping tabs on me?"

Luna's heart skipped a beat at the sound of her name. Jordan showed up because I was here? her mind raced.

"Of course I knew. I even knew you'd bring her back to your office. Remember, I know you better than you know yourself," Jordan said, her voice dripping with confidence.

Myra stiffened, a moment of silence stretching between them. "Just type your letter," she said, unlocking herself from Jordan's hold.

"At the front desk, please," she added, her voice firm, almost too controlled.

"Fine," Jordan snapped, her tone annoyed, but she didn't argue.

Myra walked back into her office, and Luna, still standing by the door, could feel her heart racing. She was too caught up in the tension between Myra and Jordan to focus on anything else.

"I'm sorry about that. She's…" Myra started as she re-entered the office.

"I can tell she's jealous. See me as competition?" Luna asked, her voice steady, cutting through the heaviness in the room.

Myra nodded but avoided Luna's gaze. She chewed her bottom lip nervously. "I guess I'll give you the backstory now."

Luna's curiosity was piqued, but before Myra could continue, Luna's voice softened. "How come you never tried to contact me?"

Myra let out a long sigh, as if she had been holding this back for years. She hesitated before speaking, her eyes wandering the room as if searching for the right words.

"Because I felt like I was the last person you wanted to talk to after I left," Myra said quietly, her voice tinged with guilt. "The way I just left—it was a big part of it. I know I should have told you. I know I should have said something before I left."

"Myra, that was the least you could have done. If anybody should have known, it should have been me, as close as we were." Luna's voice cracked with emotion. "You used to tell me everything. But that you didn't tell me?" Her words were heavy, a mix of anger and hurt.

Myra's gaze flickered to Luna's, and for a moment, something shifted between them. She looked away quickly, breaking the eye contact, and focused on the floor. Her hands tightened at her sides, betraying her unease.

"Are there any other reasons you didn't tell me you were leaving?" Luna asked, her tone soft but probing.

Myra let out another long sigh, and the room fell silent. She seemed to weigh the decision of whether to open up completely. Finally, she spoke, her voice barely above a whisper.

"I couldn't tell you, Luna. Not yet."

Her words lingered in the air as the tension thickened. Luna said nothing. But the way her shoulders stiffened, the way her breath caught for just a second—she blinked slowly, trying to swallow the rising lump in her throat.

That said enough.

Chapter 3
Almost Love, Always Running

The hours spent talking with Luna back then had been some of the hardest and best—late nights filled with frustration, honesty, and advice Myra wasn't ready to hear. Luna's words had always cut deep, and the one that still echoed in Myra's mind was the one that hurt the most: "Myra, I just don't see it. Nicole isn't serious about you. You've got to let go, move on, and stop holding on to something that doesn't seem real."

Those words clawed at her, replaying on an endless loop, haunting her in the quiet moments. But Myra wasn't ready to accept them—not yet.

Even now, in the stillness of her thoughts, Myra fought against those words, trying to dismiss them. How could she let go when everything in her heart told her the connection with Nicole wasn't just some fleeting spark? How could she move on when the memory of their first meeting still burned so brightly in her mind?

Myra let her mind drift to the night it all began.

The memory was clear, vivid even, as if it had happened just yesterday. She remembered the night she met Nicole, a night that had started out chaotic and confusing but had shifted into something she couldn't forget.

It was a sultry summer evening, the kind where the air hummed with energy and the promise of something more. Myra and her best friend, Jayy, had decided to embrace the madness, diving headfirst into the lively chaos of a foam party.

They arrived at a scene straight out of a dream: colorful lights flashing like shooting stars, pulsating beats vibrating through their bodies, and a sea of laughter swirling around them as they waded through thick, frothy bubbles that clung to their skin.

Earlier that week, Myra had been casually talking to a girl she met through mutual friends—one of those situations that looked good on paper but lacked any real spark. The chemistry just wasn't there, and no matter how much the girl tried to force deeper conversations or cling to Myra's attention, Myra felt herself emotionally checking out. Still, the girl showed up at the party uninvited, hoping to "fix things," and it didn't take long before they were caught in a heated back-and-forth in the middle of the dance floor.

Myra was already dealing with a situation she wasn't even into, and now they were tangled in yet another argument. Frustration simmered beneath her skin, but then, like a beacon in the chaos, Myra spotted Nicole—her blue hair shimmering like an ethereal halo amidst the madness. In that moment, something shifted inside her, pulling her forward.

It was reckless, but she'd done it anyway. To provoke jealousy in the girl she was with, Myra strode up to the vibrant stranger and wrapped her arms around her in a warm embrace, as if they were long-lost friends reunited after years apart. The world around them faded, and all that mattered was the thrill of the moment, the spark of something new that had taken root inside her.

Myra could still feel the heat of that night, the rush of doing something unexpected. The foam, the music, the lights—it had all been a blur, but Nicole stood out, an anchor in the storm.

From that night on, everything with Nicole moved quickly. What started as a spark at a foam party turned into constant texts and sneaking out late just to be near each other. Their chemistry was undeniable, and somewhere between laughs, secrets and stolen moments, Myra slipped into something that felt like love—fast, reckless, and hard to define. As summer crept in and campus began to clear out, Myra missed the deadline to secure housing for the next term. Technically, she could have stayed with her grandparents who lived nearby, but her relationship with her grandfather was strained, and the thought of going back home felt heavier than staying lost. That's when Nicole's mom stepped in.

She barely knew Myra, but after one phone call and a quiet conversation, she offered her a place to stay until things were figured out. It wasn't ideal, but it felt better than being adrift. So, with Nicole already back at school, Myra took her mom up on the offer.

One night, as Myra drove back to Nicole's mom's house from work, she thought about Luna. She hadn't told Luna about her living situation. She hadn't told anyone, really. Not because it was something to hide, but because it was all too confusing. It was hard enough to face her own emotions.

The truth was, Myra had known deep down that she had feelings for Luna. She'd always known. It wasn't just the late-night talks or the way Luna could cut through her uncertainty like a knife. It was the way Luna's presence made her feel grounded, seen, heard. But at the time, Myra was with Nicole. It wasn't supposed to be a choice. It wasn't supposed to be a complication. She couldn't entertain the idea of Luna like that, not while she was trying to figure out her relationship with Nicole. But that didn't stop the guilt from creeping in. Every time Luna laughed, every time she offered Myra comfort without condition, Myra felt like she was stealing something that didn't belong to her—taking warmth from someone she couldn't give herself to. Not then. Not fully. They had never spoken about what was clearly unspoken between them, what Myra had come to realize only after she'd already been tangled up with Nicole. She couldn't shake the feeling that Luna, as perceptive as she was, might have known. But Luna never let on.

There was no confrontation, no confession, just an understanding that Myra would make her choices, however complicated.

But there had been one night.

It was one of their usual late-night talks, the kind that stretched lazily into the early hours, where time seemed to fold in on itself. The overhead light was off, leaving the room bathed in the warm, orange glow of the bedside lamp. Luna's bed was a chaotic mess of mismatched pillows and a blanket that barely covered the both of them. Myra sat cross-legged, her knee just brushing against Luna's thigh as she talked animatedly about some half- forgotten childhood memory. Luna laughed, her head tilting back in that way that always caught Myra off guard, like the sound of it filled the entire room.

Myra shook the memory away, but it clung to her like static. She wondered if Luna ever thought about that night, if she even remembered it at all. Knowing her, she probably did, but true to form, she never brought it up.

When summer ended, Nicole packed up and headed back to school, three hours away in Nashville. Myra stayed behind, trying to figure out her next steps, unsure of what exactly they were to each other now that their days weren't spent tangled up in the same city. What had felt intense and intimate over the summer started to stretch thin. The distance made everything harder to hold onto.

At first, Nicole came across as gracious but distant, always preoccupied with family troubles, the pressures of school, and a fragile connection with Myra that never quite found balance. It had been a bit of a mess, to say the least. The long-distance thing wasn't easy. The three-hour drive between campuses turned their relationship into something fragmented, more texting than talking, more missed calls than shared moments. The silence between them often felt heavier than the distance.

Even when Myra tried to push past it, to ignore the growing distance, there was always that nagging thought in the back of her mind.

Maybe it was easier to stay with someone who didn't ask her to bare it all. Nicole didn't press. She didn't dig. And for someone like Myra, who'd spent most of her life hiding behind ambition and charm that felt safer than being seen by someone like Luna. Still, the quiet between them grew louder with every week. Their conversations felt routine, surface-level, like placeholders for something that used to be deeper. Myra tried to convince herself that love didn't have to be intense to be real, but even that felt like a lie some days. She began to wonder if Nicole truly saw her, or if she was just there—easy to reach and easy to be with because she didn't ask for more.

Was she just convenient? Someone to pass the time until Nicole figured it out? They'd fought more in those few months than in the entire time they'd been together, and it didn't help that their lives seemed to be moving in different directions.

And yet, Myra stayed.

Then came the day Nicole finally needed Myra in a way that felt real.

Her phone buzzed while she was folding laundry in the dim light of her bedroom. The name Nicole lit up her screen, and for a moment, she considered ignoring it. But something in her gut told her to answer.

"Hey," Myra said, trying to sound casual.

Nicole didn't waste time. "I can't do this on my own," she said, her voice low and tight. "I need you to help me get settled in at school."

Myra paused, thrown by the directness. "Wait, like… come to Nashville?"

"Yes. I have the apartment keys you helped me get, but no car, no one to help move the boxes, no idea how I'm going to do this without you." Nicole let out a breath. "I know things have been weird between us, but… I need you."

Myra sank onto the edge of the bed, laundry forgotten. Her chest tightened, but not in a bad way. This wasn't just another call. It felt like an invitation, maybe even a turning point.

"Okay," she said after a beat. "I'll come."

With the promise of an apartment waiting for her, Myra had taken the leap: three hours away, to a campus where she'd never been, to a place where her presence would no longer be an afterthought.

The drive had been quiet, just Myra and her thoughts, each mile peeling back layers of uncertainty. She gripped the wheel tighter every time her mind drifted back to Luna—how she never told her best friend she was leaving, how she didn't explain anything. Myra had shut down the moment things with Nicole got serious, pulling away from the one person who might have truly understood her.

Maybe that was the difference.

Nicole loved her in bursts. When things were good, they were magnetic: all laughter and heat and long glances. But when things got hard, Nicole disappeared. She didn't ask questions. She didn't press. And in some twisted way, Myra had convinced herself that was easier—that not being seen was safer.

But Luna? Luna had always seen her. Even in silence. Even when Myra tried to pretend there was nothing there.

Their love—if you could call it that—had always lived in the in- between. Not quite romantic, not just friendship, but something charged and wordless. Something Myra never dared touch because she already knew: if she let herself feel that fully, there'd be no going back.

So, she stayed with Nicole. Not because it was right, but because it asked less of her.

And she knew it. The distance wasn't just physical, it had been emotional, deliberate. Even now, hours and months removed, she could feel the ache of that silence.

If Luna had known—if Myra had told her, or shown up at her door one last time before she left—maybe things would have gone differently.

Maybe Myra would have stayed.

Maybe she would have said everything she was too scared to say out loud. That it wasn't just comfort, or closeness. It was more.

But Myra wasn't ready.

Not for a love that held a mirror to her.

Not for someone who would challenge her when she shut down.

Not for someone who could see through her every excuse and still wait for the truth. Luna had always seen her too clearly.

And that kind of love, accountable and intense, was something Myra had never known how to receive.

So she ran.

Not just because she was afraid of being loved like that, but because deep down, she didn't even know if Luna felt the same. And the thought of being fully seen, and unchosen? That was a heartbreak she wasn't willing to risk.

When she finally pulled into the narrow lot behind the small apartment complex, the sun was already beginning to dip. Nashville buzzed faintly in the distance, unfamiliar but not unwelcoming.

Nicole met her at the door, a mix of relief and tension in her eyes. There weren't many words exchanged—just a brief hug, a quiet thank you, and the unmistakable weight of things left unsaid.

Inside, the apartment was mostly bare. A few boxes were scattered in the living room. An air mattress leaned against the wall. It wasn't much, but it was something.

Myra set down her bag, feeling the weight of it all settle in her chest. The doubts, the fears, the lingering hurt—they all existed in this space. But so did the hope, the excitement, and the possibility of something more.

They had a lot to work through, a lot of miscommunications to unpack. But as they stood in this space together, Myra felt a flicker of something different.

They would figure it out, one day at a time.

CHAPTER 4
I SHOULD'VE
CHANGED THE LOCKS

Nicole and Myra's relationship had always been complicated, but not in the classic sense. There wasn't a tragic misunderstanding or unfortunate timing. Instead, their complications crept in silently, weaving themselves deeper until Myra found herself struggling just to breathe.

At first, Nicole seemed perfectly captivating—confident, magnetic. She had a way of making Myra feel like she was the only person who mattered. Myra poured herself into Nicole, determined to show her love in every imaginable way. Myra loved fiercely and without limits. Flowers for no reason, surprise lunches at work, random gifts just to see Nicole smile—she poured into her every way she knew how. And she never stopped, even when she should have.

Nicole was always posting and sharing moments online for attention. So, of course, one day she posted a photo of the two of them on Instagram, making sure everyone knew they were together. A mirror selfie from weeks before, both in hoodies, Myra's arm tucked into Nicole's waist. The caption read, *"my calm in the chaos"* with a heart emoji.

Myra reread it three times before smiling. It felt like confirmation, like even if Nicole didn't always say it out loud, she still saw her. Still wanted her. That single post carried Myra through a lot of things she shouldn't have forgiven.

She once came home with a delicate gold ring. Nothing extravagant—just a thin band, no stone, a quiet little loop she picked up from a pop-up kiosk near the food court.

"Saw it and thought of you," Nicole said, dropping the tiny box on the bed like it cost her nothing. Myra wore it every day. Not because she loved the ring, but because it gave her something to believe in—something to point to when people asked, *"Why are you still with her?"*

It looked like a promise, even if none had been made.

There were other moments too. Like the time Nicole introduced her to her friends at that rooftop party, fingers laced with Myra's, proudly calling her *"my girl"* loud enough for everyone to hear. Myra's heart had thudded against her ribs like it was trying to memorize the moment. For weeks afterward, she replayed it like a favorite song—the way Nicole's arm had rested on her lower back, the way people looked at them. She hadn't felt invisible. Not that night.

But soon, cracks began to appear.

Nicole loved control more than anything else, and slowly Myra found herself losing her voice. Every choice, from where they ate dinner to how they spent their weekends, was made by Nicole. Whenever Myra expressed her wishes, Nicole would dismiss them with a wave of her hand or a mocking laugh.

Eventually, Myra stopped speaking up, choosing peace over her own happiness.

She still did the dishes. She still made sure Nicole had a packed lunch. Still paid the light bill. Still rearranged her work schedule to be available when Nicole needed her. She didn't mind providing. She minded never being poured into.

Myra told herself this was love—that bending, compromising, keeping the peace meant she was doing it right. She'd grown up believing that loving someone meant shrinking yourself when things got uncomfortable. So that's what she did. She made herself smaller.

And when she finally started stepping into herself—painting her nails, wearing softer fabrics, taking selfies that made her feel pretty—Nicole looked at her like she'd turned into a stranger.

"You didn't used to be like this," Nicole had said one night, eyes narrowed.

Myra laughed nervously, tucking a curl behind her ear. *"Like what?"*

"Girly. Extra. Like… you're trying to get attention or something."

It was supposed to be a joke, but it didn't feel like one.

Soon, the silence between who Myra really was and who Nicole needed her to become grew unbearable.

Then the jealousy started. Innocent conversations turned into battles. Nicole questioned Myra relentlessly, convinced she was hiding something.

One night at a crowded bar, everything spiraled out of control. The music thumped inside, a bassline so heavy Myra could feel it in her chest. She had just finished a harmless conversation with a girl at the bar—nothing flirty, just a shared laugh about their identical boots. But when she turned around, she caught Nicole's glare from across the room.

Myra's stomach dropped. She knew that look.

Before she could take a step, Nicole was already beside her, fingers gripping her wrist.

"What the fuck was that?" Nicole hissed, yanking her through the crowd and shoving open the bar's back door into the night.

The cold air bit into Myra's skin. "Nicole, what's going on?"

"Don't play dumb with me. You were all in that girl's face. Laughing. Smiling. You think I didn't see that shit?"

"Wait, what? I was literally talking about shoes. That's all."

"Shoes?" Nicole scoffed, her voice rising. *"You think I'm fucking blind?"*

Myra pulled her wrist back. *"You're overreacting."*

"Don't gaslight me."

"I'm not. I'm trying to explain."

"I see you, Myra. You have been different lately. More makeup. New clothes. Acting brand new."

That stopped Myra cold.

"So now me feeling good about myself is a threat to you?"

Nicole laughed bitterly. *"No. But it's funny how you never looked like that when we first met."*

Myra swallowed hard. *"Maybe you just didn't pay attention then."*

Still, Myra wondered if she had gone too far. Maybe the selfies were a little extra. Maybe she should've eased into the changes. Was it wrong to want to feel beautiful without needing permission?

That night, Myra found herself apologizing repeatedly for a mistake she never made, tears quietly slipping down her cheeks as she tried to convince Nicole of her innocence. Yet Nicole's own actions never faced the same scrutiny.

She kept asking herself what she could've done differently. Should she have laughed quieter? Not made eye contact with the girl? She replayed the interaction over and over, searching for where she might've gone wrong.

That night, Myra didn't just cry because of Nicole's anger, she cried because a part of her believed it. The way Nicole twisted the narrative made her second-guess her own memories, her own feelings, her own self.

There was a moment she knew this wasn't love, not the way love should feel. But the fear of starting over felt bigger than the fear of being unloved. This wasn't just a fight, it was the beginning of Myra questioning her own reality. And when your reality feels unstable, everything else crumbles with it. The next morning, Nicole brought Myra breakfast in bed. It wasn't much: two slices of dry toast, orange juice in a cracked mug. Still, she placed it down carefully, then kissed Myra's forehead like nothing had happened.

"I was drunk," Nicole mumbled. *"And you know I get jealous. That's on me."*

Myra nodded, even though it wasn't enough. It wasn't an apology. It was an explanation with no weight behind it. But the toast was warm. And her lips were soft. And for a few seconds, Myra pretended that meant something.

Myra supported Nicole in many things, including her dream of becoming a model. As her modeling career began to take off, it brought late-night photo sessions and endless excuses. Myra often woke up alone, Nicole's side of the bed cold and untouched. When confronted, Nicole would roll her eyes dismissively. *"It's work. Stop being insecure, Myra."*

She tried not to spiral. Maybe she was being too sensitive. Maybe she just didn't understand the demands of modeling.

She hated how easily she questioned herself these days, but it felt safer than accusing Nicole and being wrong.

Then came the parade of questionable "friends"—so-called photographers and party promoters introduced casually as *"brothers,"* but whose glances lingered too long, whose smiles carried secretive meanings Myra couldn't ignore.

It was a Friday night. Myra had lit candles in the living room, her favorite playlist humming low in the background. She made dinner, nothing fancy, just something warm. But the plate on the other side of the table sat untouched. Nicole had been "out with her friends" since six. It was nearly midnight now.

Myra picked up her phone and typed:

Myra: *Hey, what time do you think you'll be back?*

Maybe she'd misread the evening. Maybe Nicole just needed space and Myra was doing too much. She checked the plates again, wondering if she should have made something else. Something Nicole liked more.

Myra checked her phone again. No response.

Myra: *I miss you. We barely spend time together anymore.*

Three dots appeared. Then disappeared. Finally, a reply buzzed through.

Nicole: *I'm just out. Damn. You always tripping.*

Myra swallowed hard, her fingers trembling as she typed again.

Myra: *I'm not asking for a ring, Nicole. I just want time. You don't even look at me anymore. You don't ask how my day was. You're always gone.*

The reply came almost immediately.

Myra stared at the screen, her heart sinking like a stone.

It wasn't that she wanted a proposal. She just wanted a presence. To feel wanted. To matter to the person she gave everything to. Was that too much?

But maybe she had expected too much. Maybe this was just how relationships looked for people their age. She'd never been good at being casual, and sometimes she worried that made her hard to love.

She didn't respond to the text message. There was nothing left to say.

For the first time, she looked around her apartment and truly saw it. The bills were in her name. The lease was hers. The food in the fridge, the lights on, the Wi-Fi Nicole used to post stories with her "friends"… all paid for by Myra.

And yet, she was sitting here, waiting like a fool. Waiting for someone who didn't even check in, who couldn't even lie right.

That was the moment something shifted. Myra didn't say it aloud, but in her head, she heard it clear as day: *I should've changed the locks.*

She didn't. Not yet. But she started mentally packing Nicole's things, folding up the parts of herself she had given away for free. Reclaiming them.

Eventually, Jayy, Myra's best friend, shattered the fragile trust she had left. Sitting in a quiet coffee shop, his face full of pain, he gently revealed what he'd seen.

Myra had been spiraling for weeks, brushing off her gut instincts. But Jayy—her best friend and mirror—had been watching her break in silence. One day, he couldn't take it anymore.

"Myra, Nicole slept with someone else. I saw her leave with him myself."

Myra's world came crashing down around her. She confronted Nicole, demanding answers, only to be met with more empty promises and tears.

"Myra, it was nothing. It'll never happen again. I'll change, I promise. I love you," Nicole begged.

And Myra, desperate to hold onto what they'd once had, believed her again.

Myra gave everything, and Nicole took it all for granted.

Take Nicole's birthday, for instance. The room smelled like candles and fried food, champagne and last-minute perfume. Balloons floated unevenly, tethered to chairs and door handles. The lights were dimmed just enough to feel intentional, but not so low that the flaws couldn't be seen.

Myra stood near the kitchen, eyes darting between the front door and the time on her phone. Her heart raced behind her ribcage— not out of anxiety, but something deeper. She wanted this to go right. She needed it to go right.

This night was her offering. Her proof.

She was still trying to earn her place. Still hoping that if she showed up big enough, loved loud enough, Nicole would remember what made her stay in the first place.

That she still loved Nicole enough to fight for them. Even if things had been tense lately—words unsaid, touch missing, emotions sharp—she still believed in them. She always had.

She had coordinated everything: the food, the friends, the playlist that was probably too soft, the last-minute cash she dropped to fly a few people in. She didn't care. It was worth it.

Because when Myra loved, she didn't do it halfway.

The room was filled with chatter. People were sipping, eating, whispering. But underneath it all, there was something off. Myra couldn't place it. A flicker in the way someone looked at her and turned away. A joke that seemed aimed but never landed. Eyes shifting too quickly when she glanced their way.

Still, she pushed through it. Tonight wasn't about her.

It was for Nicole.

And then the door opened.

"SURPRISE!"

The yell nearly knocked the air out of the room.

Nicole froze in the doorway, eyes wide, lips parted—the kind of expression that teetered between joy and shock.

Then she smiled.

And Myra smiled back, relief flooding her bones.

But there was something else behind Nicole's eyes. Something Myra saw, even if she didn't want to. A flicker. A delay in the way she reached for her, like she had to remind herself to respond.

The hug was warm, but Myra felt the pause—that hesitation just before arms wrapped around her.

Nicole whispered, "You did all this?"

Myra grinned and nodded. "Of course I did. For you."

She didn't see the way Nicole's smile faltered for half a second, or how she swallowed too hard. But her spirit did.

The night unfolded with polite laughter and offbeat conversations.

People mingled, took selfies, poured drinks. Myra flitted between groups, topping off cups, refilling trays. She was glowing, trying to hold everything together—the event, the mood, the love.

And Nicole?

She was trying too.

But her laughter was too loud. Her eye contact too rehearsed. She glanced at her phone more than she should have. And in the moments when she thought no one was watching, she looked tired of pretending.

Because the truth was loud in her body, even if her mouth stayed quiet.

Nicole and her best friends retreated upstairs.

Paige closed the bathroom door behind her and locked it with a click that sounded louder than she intended. Rae sat on the edge of the garden tub, checking her lashes in a handheld mirror.

Nicole stood at the sink, twisting a gold hoop back into place.

"Y'all know I don't like surprises," Nicole said, her voice playful but tired.

Paige raised an eyebrow. "Girl, we flew in for you. We deserve Oscars."

Rae laughed. "For real. But Myra? She really did all this?"

Nicole didn't answer right away. She just looked at herself in the mirror—the soft curve of her jaw, the faint dark circles under her eyes. She looked pretty. She looked tired. She looked like she was pretending.

Paige noticed.

"You good?" she asked gently.

Nicole leaned closer to the mirror, adjusting her baby hairs.

"Yeah."

Rae scoffed. "No, you not. You been weird all day. Real quiet."

Paige cut in. "Tell the truth—this whole thing feel too much? Like... you not tryna play house with Myra, are you?"

Nicole flinched. Just a little. But enough.

Rae sat up straighter. "I'm serious. You been acting funny ever since... well, you know." She motioned vaguely toward Nicole's stomach.

The silence thickened.

Paige frowned. "Wait. You really went through with it?"

Nicole swallowed hard. "I didn't have a choice. I couldn't..." She didn't finish the sentence. Instead, she turned the faucet on full blast, like it might drown out her voice. "Don't bring that up tonight."

Rae shifted uncomfortably. "We're not judging. Just... you ain't tell Myra, did you?"

Nicole's voice was soft. "No. I couldn't."

Paige leaned against the door. "That girl is downstairs planning your future like she already married you."

"She would've kept it," Rae whispered. Nicole nodded.

"She would've rearranged her whole life if she knew."

Paige sighed. "That's the thing. She loves you too hard. And you keep letting her."

Nicole blinked quickly. "I'm not ready for that kind of love."

No one said anything after that. Because it was true.

She knew she didn't deserve this night.

Not with what she'd been doing behind Myra's back. Not with the way she'd been disappearing emotionally.

And not with the things she'd whispered to others when Myra wasn't around.

At one point, Myra stepped out to grab something—napkins maybe, or a lighter. And that's when it happened.

The room quieted. Just for a moment. Someone whispered, "She don't even know..." Another voice snorted.

Someone else changed the subject too quickly, too obviously.

When Myra walked back in, the tension broke. People laughed too hard. Smiles returned, bright and brittle.

She felt it. But she said nothing.

Later, Myra and Nicole stood together in a corner of the room. Myra had her arm around Nicole's waist.

Nicole leaned in.

But her eyes… her eyes were gone.

Myra stared at her, trying to memorize the shape of her smile. Trying to believe this night meant something. That it fixed what felt broken.

But deep down, her spirit knew. This wasn't a celebration.

It was a goodbye in disguise.

As the night wound down and people hugged them goodbye, someone whispered in Myra's ear:

"You're a good one. For real."

It was the way they said it, solemn, like a eulogy, that made her stomach twist.

In the quiet hours after everyone left, when balloons had started to sag and the music had died, Myra lay next to Nicole in silence.

Nicole said, "Thank you again. I loved tonight."

And Myra just nodded, staring at the ceiling, blinking back tears she didn't understand yet.

She didn't know her spirit had already begun preparing her heart for what would come next.

She kept giving because giving distracted her.

She knew she was being mistreated, but creating moments of joy gave her something to hold onto.

A high to chase.

Loving Nicole was starting to feel like a drug. It numbed her, even while it hollowed her out. For a while after the party, things were calm.

Or maybe Myra just stopped noticing the storm.

But when Myra's own birthday came around, she hadn't been sure what she wanted to do. She kept it vague on purpose, partly because she didn't want to seem high maintenance, but mostly because she was hoping Nicole would take the lead.

Not with some over-the-top spectacle, just intention. Something personal. Something soft.

A dinner reservation. A letter.

Even just the effort of planning without being asked.

So when Nicole asked, "What you tryna do for your birthday?" Myra shrugged and said, "I don't know yet." But what she really meant was, *Surprise me, but don't forget who I am.*

Instead, a party flyer started making the rounds on Instagram. Black and silver graphics, three-day weekend lineup, out-of-town DJs, free before 11 PM. Myra kept seeing it. Over and over.

When she scrolled past it again that Wednesday, Nicole casually called out from the bathroom.

"Oh, I forgot to tell you. That party's this weekend. My folks from Atlanta and Dallas coming in town. We're all sliding through."

Myra looked up from her phone slowly. "This weekend?"

Nicole reappeared in the doorway, drying her hands. "Yeah. That big party. Same weekend as your birthday, right?" She said it like the overlap was inconvenient, not obvious. "But we can still go to brunch or something. Sunday maybe?"

No mention of Myra coming to the party. No ticket bought. No plan to include her.

The decision had already been made.

Myra didn't say anything. She just nodded slowly and looked back down at her phone. She could feel the air pull tight between them, but Nicole didn't notice. Or didn't care.

On the night of her birthday, Myra got dressed in silence. A dark fitted dress.

Gold jewelry.

She curled her hair, added gloss, sprayed perfume like armor.

Her phone buzzed with casual wishes from people she barely spoke to. Nothing from Nicole.

No *"Hey, you still wanna do something later?"*

No *"Let's at least grab dessert."*

At 8:42 PM, Myra texted Nicole a single line:

"You still going out tonight?"

Nicole replied fifteen minutes later:

"Yeah, we pre-gaming at Paige's. Everybody already lit lol."

No mention of her birthday.

No "You wanna come?"

Just vibes that didn't include her.

So Myra made a decision.

She called Kay, her coworker, and asked if their offer to "take her out if Nicole flaked" was still good. Twenty minutes later, she was in an Uber, her stomach hollow and her chest tight.

They went to a bar first—a cozy gay spot with cheap drinks and neon signs. Then a club. Her friends bought rounds. They hyped her up. She danced. Laughed. Took blurry photos. Pretended the ache in her throat was from the tequila.

But around 1 AM, standing under purple lights while a remix thumped through the speakers, Myra leaned against the wall and stared at her phone. Still no text. No call. Not even a lazy *"Happy birthday."*

And that's when it hit her.

She's not busy. She's just not thinking about me.

Because when it was her birthday, Myra made it a whole production. And when it was hers, Nicole went to pregame.

But still, Myra wondered if she'd made it hard to celebrate her. She hadn't been clear about what she wanted. Maybe that was her fault. Maybe if she'd spoken up, Nicole would've shown up.

The next day, Nicole threw her a surprise party. If you could even call it that.

She texted Myra to "come by real quick." No explanation. When Myra walked in, a weak "Surprise" floated up from five of Nicole's friends on the couch. One of them was high, another barely looked up from her phone.

A cake sat on the counter, the kind with plastic balloon rings from a grocery store bakery. Red cups. Half a bottle of peach vodka.

Myra just stood there, keys in her hand, blinking like she'd walked into the wrong room. Nicole came up behind her and wrapped an arm around her waist.

"See? I ain't forget."

Myra forced a smile and said thank you. She sat on the couch. Took a sip of something flat. Let them sing. Let Nicole kiss her cheek.

But she could feel it. This wasn't for her. It was a performance, slapped together out of guilt. None of her people were there.

Not one of her favorite songs played. No card. No thought. No intimacy.

Just Nicole's guilt trying to shape-shift into celebration.

And it almost worked. Until one of Nicole's friends handed her a plate and said, "Hope you don't mind we kind of just threw this together last minute. Nicole's been stressed."

Myra nodded slowly and said nothing. Because what was left to say? This was supposed to be her birthday.

But somehow, she'd ended up hosting her own grief.

Myra spent days hoping. Even after all the fights, the cold shoulders, the things left unsaid, some part of her still believed today would be different. It was Valentine's Day. The one day Nicole might show up for her the way she always showed up for Nicole.

By 7 PM, nothing. No texts. No calls. Myra was curled on the couch, trying to talk herself out of crying when the door finally creaked open.

"Hey," Nicole said, walking in with a plastic bag. Myra sat up. "Hey…"

Nicole plopped the bag on the coffee table and pulled out a red teddy bear and a box of chocolates.

"Happy Valentine's," she said, kissing Myra on the cheek. Myra stared at the bear. It still had a CVS sticker on it.

"Thanks…" she mumbled, picking up the chocolates. She turned them over. Almond truffles.

"You don't like those?"

"You didn't even know what candy I like. After everything, you had to ask a stranger to pretend you were paying attention?"

Nicole raised a brow. "It's not that serious."

Myra's throat tightened. "To you, maybe."

She hated how small her voice sounded. Like a child trying to explain why her feelings mattered. Maybe she should've just said thank you and left it at that.

Myra had considered breaking up with Nicole countless times, but fear held her back. Fear of loneliness, of losing comfort, of starting over. Fear of admitting she'd poured her heart into someone who barely acknowledged her existence.

Myra sat curled on the couch, eyes heavy from another sleepless night. Her body ached from emotional exhaustion, and all she wanted, just once, was for Nicole to see her. To know her. There were nights Myra lay next to Nicole, staring at the ceiling, wondering if she was the problem. If her need for softness, for reciprocity, made her too much. She'd heard it before in different ways: she was intense, dramatic, hard to please. The voices of past hurts echoed louder whenever Nicole turned cold.

Nicole walked in, holding a takeout bag with a proud grin. "Babe, I got your favorite—veggie deluxe with olives."

Myra blinked, confused. "Olives?"

Nicole dropped the box on the coffee table, kissing Myra's forehead like she'd done something thoughtful. "Yeah, you said you liked it."

Myra opened the box slowly, the smell hitting her before she even looked. Mushrooms. Olives. No pepperoni in sight.

Myra's chest tightened. "Nicole… I hate olives."

Nicole laughed it off, grabbing a slice. "Really? You sure? I swear you mentioned this before."

"No, Nicole. I didn't." Her voice was small, almost hollow. "My favorite pizza has always been pepperoni."

The silence that followed wasn't loud—it was worse. It was the quiet that confirms a fear, the kind that says: *you never really saw me.*

The final breaking point was Monica. Myra discovered messages on Nicole's phone late one night—intimate, explicit, undeniably real. But as she read further, her heart slowed. Something was off. The words, the phrasing… this wasn't a woman. Monica didn't even sound like a woman.

A memory clawed its way back: that night at a party, Nicole whispering with a tall guy she'd never introduced, laughing too low, gone too long. Myra had asked about him.

"That's Monica," Nicole had said with a lazy grin. Myra hadn't questioned it—until now. Monica was a cover name. For a man.

Myra's stomach twisted as the full weight of the betrayal settled in her chest. Not just the cheating, but the lies, the gaslighting, the disrespect.

"Who is Monica, Nicole?" Myra asked, holding the phone up.

Her voice didn't even shake—it cracked.

Nicole faltered, guilt stretching across her face. "It's nothing, Myra."

"You lied again! After everything I've done for you, every sacrifice I've made, every time I forgave you!" Myra shouted, sobbing openly. "Flowers, lunches, parties, surprises—I did everything! You couldn't even remember my favorite chocolate without asking someone else!"

Nicole stood silent, her face expressionless, offering no genuine apology, only empty promises Myra no longer believed.

"I can't fix this by myself anymore," Myra whispered, exhausted, broken.

Nicole didn't say anything. She didn't chase her. Didn't apologize. Just stood there blank, as if nothing Myra said had ever meant anything at all.

Myra grabbed her keys and left.

She didn't know where she was going until she pulled into Jayy's driveway. She texted him from the car: Can I crash on your couch tonight?

He opened the door without a word, holding out a blanket like he'd been expecting her. Myra collapsed into the couch cushions, still in the clothes she had argued in, still shaking. Jayy didn't ask questions. He just sat nearby, letting the silence hold what she couldn't say out loud.

She didn't sleep much. Her thoughts kept running in circles. Even after all of that, all the yelling, the betrayal, the silence, part of her still hoped Nicole would text. Would call. Would show up.

She didn't.

The next morning, Myra drove back to the apartment. Her stomach turned as she pulled into the parking space. Everything looked the same, but nothing felt safe.

Myra sat with the ugliest question: *Was I so easy to lie to? Was my love that disposable?* And worse... *did I teach her it was okay to treat me this way?*

She couldn't stop wondering if she had trained Nicole to treat her this way—by staying, by forgiving, by folding herself into someone unrecognizable just to keep the peace.

She packed in silence. Each item was filled with memories of shattered dreams and endless disappointments. Tears streamed down her face as she realized she was leaving behind someone she had given her entire heart to. She kept trying to intellectualize it, to dissect what had gone wrong. But some things weren't logical. Some things just hurt. And no amount of journaling, overthinking, or replaying memories could explain why someone who once swore they loved you could also be the person who shattered you.

As she packed, Myra paused for a moment and touched the ring on her finger. She hadn't even noticed she was still wearing it. It had become second skin. A memory disguised as jewelry. She thought about taking it off. She even pulled at it slightly, twisting it at the base like she was warming up to the idea. But her hands stopped short.

It wasn't about Nicole anymore. It was about everything Myra had tried to believe. Everything she thought love was supposed to look like. Some wounds don't bleed out all at once. Some drip slowly, quietly. She would take it off. Just... not tonight.

Stepping outside the apartment for the last time, she closed the door softly behind her, leaving the echoes of a love she now knew had never truly existed.

As she sat behind the wheel of her car, tears blurred her vision. She felt utterly lost. Her thoughts raced with memories of Nicole, her heart aching with the weight of betrayal and neglect. She missed the version of herself that hadn't learned to stay quiet just to keep someone else from leaving. The version of herself before loving Nicole made her question her worth. Before every argument taught her how to say I'm fine when she wasn't. She didn't even recognize her reflection anymore. Too many compromises. Too many cracks.

Days passed in an agonizing blur. Work became a distraction from the emptiness that consumed her. Reaching out to friends felt pointless. They weren't Luna.

Wandering through the apartment complex she managed, Myra found herself drawn to an isolated unit, hidden away from the rest. It felt like a fresh start, a place untouched by memories of heartbreak.

Gathering her things from the apartment she had shared with Nicole, each item painfully symbolic, she felt a sense of finality. She had given so much, loved so deeply, fought endlessly— but it was over.

Myra sat in the car for a long time, not turning the key. Just breathing. Just sitting with the silence she had fought so hard to avoid. For years, she had convinced herself that giving love meant being swallowed whole. That love required pain. That if she just loved hard enough, Nicole would finally see her.

But love wasn't supposed to feel like drowning. And now, with nothing left to give, she finally realized... she deserved more than empty promises and half-effort affection.

She looked at her reflection in the rearview mirror—eyes swollen, face streaked with tears—and whispered. Her fingers hovered over Nicole's contact. For a second, she almost hit the call button. But some wounds didn't need closure. They needed distance.

"No more."

Driving away, the night air cooled against her skin. Clarity slowly rose from beneath the pain: For so long, Myra thought love meant proving herself. Shrinking. Bleeding. But now she knew, love wasn't meant to undo you. It was meant to return you to yourself. And this time, she wouldn't forget who she was just to keep someone else comfortable.

She was finally choosing herself.

CHAPTER 5
YOU FORGOT ME

The key shook in her hand before it even touched the lock.

Myra stood outside her new apartment, arms heavy with the weight of her overnight bag—the duffel stuffed with skin care, journals, chargers, and pain. The movers wouldn't arrive until morning. For tonight, it was just her. A sleeping bag. And silence.

The door opened easily. No resistance. No screech. Already different from Nicole.

The air smelled clean. Almost too clean, like something had been scrubbed away that was never supposed to return.

Myra stepped in slowly. Not because she was scared, but because it felt unreal. Like this wasn't hers. Like at any moment, Nicole would text, *Come home. Let's talk.* And she'd go. Again.

But the phone stayed quiet. She dropped her bags at the threshold and stood there, staring at the space. Blank walls. White cabinets. Empty floors.

She should have felt free. But all she felt was lost.

This apartment didn't know her yet. Didn't know the sound of her laugh when she played her old playlists. Didn't know the smell of her shea butter or peppermint soap. Didn't know the tears she cried at 2 a.m. when she whispered, *I'm done,* but wasn't.

She slid down the wall and sat on the cold floor. The hardwood pressed against her spine like a truth she couldn't avoid.

This was it.

Day One.

After a long, sleepless night in her new apartment, Myra's eyes opened slowly to the bright light pouring through her curtainless windows. It was too harsh. Too honest. It didn't let her hide.

She sat up slowly, the sleeping bag sliding off her shoulders like old skin. Her body felt sore—not just from the floor, but from the weight of everything she had been carrying.

At first, she didn't know what she felt.

But the longer she sat in the stillness, the more it came roaring forward: anger.

Hot. Heavy. Unrelenting.

Not the kind that lashes out blindly, but the kind that coils in your gut and spits the truth you've been too scared to say.

Myra was angry at herself.

Angry that she saw the red flags and still painted them white.

Angry that she bent so far backward for love she didn't notice when her own spine started to crack.

She was angry for every time she told herself, It's not that bad. For every tear she wiped in secret just to keep the peace. For every silence she swallowed to keep Nicole comfortable.

She was angry for the birthdays that went unnoticed. For the lies dressed up as half-truths. For the way Nicole could look her dead in the face after betrayal and still say, *You're being dramatic.*

But the worst part?

She was angry that she let it happen. Again.

And again.

And again.

She was angry at the little girl inside her who still believed love had to be earned through suffering.

Angry at the way she made herself smaller every time Nicole needed to feel big.

Angry that she turned herself into a landing pad for Nicole's wounds while hers bled out unattended.

She was angry that she couldn't remember the last time she felt safe in her own home. That she mistook chaos for passion.

That she made excuses for someone who wouldn't even make space for her.

She was angry that Nicole never opened her damn eyes.

That someone could be loved so deeply and still choose destruction.

That Myra could give everything—time, money, her body, her soul—and it still wasn't enough to make Nicole see her.

And underneath it all, the sharpest cut:

She was angry that even now, in this brand-new space, with fresh paint and her name on the lease, Nicole still lived rent-free in her head.

Myra clenched her jaw and threw the covers off. No more lying in it.

No more pretending it was okay.

No more loyalty to her own suffering. Today, her anger had a voice.

And it wasn't asking for permission.

Her feet moved on instinct, pulling her toward the bathroom like something was calling her.

She turned on the light. There she was.

Puffy eyes.

Tear-streaked cheeks. Lips trembling. Edges frizzed.

No filters. No soft lighting to blur the truth. Just Myra.

She gripped the edge of the sink, breath uneven. Her reflection looked back at her like a stranger she used to know, someone she'd abandoned to keep a woman who never planned on staying.

Her eyes filled again, tears pushing forward without consent. She wanted to look away.

But she couldn't.

Because this was what she had been avoiding—the face of the woman who let herself disappear.

"You forgot me," she whispered to her reflection. A sob slipped out, sharp and sudden.

"You fucking forgot me."

She slammed her palm on the counter. The sound cracked through the apartment like a gunshot.

Tears came harder. Years of them. Years of pretending.

Years of forgiving too easily.

Years of thinking, maybe if I love her better, she won't break me this time.

"Look what you did to me," Myra cried, voice hoarse, chest heaving.

Not to herself. Not entirely.

To the ghost of Nicole still lingering in her bones.

To the woman in the mirror who needed to be seen again.

"I carried your pain. I held your shame. I swallowed your anger."

She slapped her chest once, hard.

"I let you turn me into someone I don't even fucking recognize!"

And then she dropped to her knees on the bathroom floor and cried until her stomach ached.

Until her breath came in gasps.

Until her chest burned from the pressure of unspoken words, uncried tears, unprocessed rage.

It wasn't pretty. It wasn't poetic. It was real.

It was the moment she stopped pretending she was okay. The moment she stopped performing strength.

The moment she said goodbye to the silence that had protected everyone but her.

Eventually, the sobs slowed. Her body trembled less.

The mirror didn't look as foreign.

Myra crawled toward it on her knees, placed both hands on the counter, looked herself dead in the eye, and whispered, "I'm still in here.

And I'm not fucking leaving me again." It didn't happen all at once.

There was no epiphany. No dramatic new me moment.

Just a quiet morning, two weeks after the mirror, when Myra made her bed. It was the first thing she completed in full.

The sheet was still wrinkled, and the throw blanket sat crooked, but it was hers. Neat. Chosen. Done.

That same morning, she sat on the edge of her bed and opened a fresh journal. Not the one she used to process her pain.

This one was blank.

Crisp pages. No triggers. No trauma. Just space.

She didn't know what to write, so she started with what she knew:

"My name is Myra.

I don't know who I am yet. But I'm willing to find out.

I know I like candles that smell like eucalyptus.

I know I cry in the shower because it feels safer than the bed.

I know I want more, even if I don't know what more looks like yet."

She didn't write every day. Some days, she just sat in silence. But the silence didn't feel so empty anymore.

It felt… sacred.

A few days later, she went for a walk without music.

Just her breath. Her heartbeat. The crunch of gravel under her sneakers. And somewhere between mile one and mile two, she whispered, "I'm proud of you."

Not loudly. Not for show. Just enough for her soul to hear it. She started a new morning ritual.

Nothing complicated. Wake up.

Make the bed. Light a candle. Journal for ten minutes.

Play a podcast that didn't talk about relationships, just growth: discipline, confidence, business.

She liked the way those words sounded in her space.

She began meditating—short ones. Five minutes. Seven if she felt brave. Sometimes she'd cry in the middle of them. Sometimes she'd fall asleep.

But other times, she'd feel her body soften in ways it never had when she was trying to be "strong."

Then came the dream.

Not the kind you have when you're asleep.

The kind that taps you on the shoulder when you're mid-podcast with oatmeal in your lap.

Real estate.

She remembered having a conversation years ago about how she was already working in property management, but wanted to take it a step further.

But Nicole wasn't as supportive of her dreams as she was of hers.

So, she shelved it, like everything else she wanted.

Not anymore.

That same day, Myra Googled local real estate schools.

She found one with flexible classes, called to ask a few questions, and by the end of the week, she was enrolled.

It scared the shit out of her.

She hadn't been a student in years. What if she failed? What if she didn't belong?

But she showed up—hoodie, notebook, water bottle, and all.

And for the first time in a long time, she felt like she was building something no one could take from her.

She started leaving Post-it notes around the apartment: affirmations, prayers, pep talks.

"I release the version of me who needed survival love." "Healing is not linear, but it's mine."

"You do not have to earn being chosen."

Each note was a seed.

Not every one bloomed, but Myra kept planting.

While her apartment was filled with affirmations, it was also covered in sticky notes with vocabulary terms and acronyms.

The mirror she once used for lashes and lip gloss now displayed a full breakdown of agency relationships.

The fridge was lined with key contract law definitions.

Her nightstand was buried in highlighters, flashcards, and open notebooks.

Even her bathroom had a sticky note taped to the toilet tank: "Title theory = lender holds the title."

Myra had turned her entire world into a study sanctuary. The first time she took the test, she failed.

By two points.

It stung, not just because she missed passing, but because it felt like a reflection of every time she'd tried to move forward and gotten pulled back.

For a moment, that old voice crept in:

You're not as ready as you think you are. But she didn't let it settle.

She sat in her car, blinking back the heat in her eyes, and whispered, "Okay. We try again."

This time, she doubled down. She rewrote every note.

Watched real estate YouTube videos like they were binge-worthy series.

Read chapters out loud to herself until she knew them by heart.

Her phone's lock screen became a daily mantra: Pass or not, you are already becoming her.

The apartment stayed cluttered—papers here, open books there—but it was sacred chaos.

She wasn't unraveling anymore.

She was rebuilding.

And then came the second try.

She walked into the testing center with a quiet calm. Not confidence exactly, more like surrender.

She knew she had done the work. That was enough.

When she saw the word PASS on the screen, her breath caught in her throat.

Myra walked out slowly, holding the paper in both hands like it might vanish if she blinked.

She didn't smile until she sat in the car.

Then the dam broke.

She cried loudly, freely. Head back, shoulders shaking, release.

Tears fell not just for the win, but for every moment before it when she wanted to give up and didn't. This wasn't about real estate.

This was about reclaiming her future.

That night, she didn't party.

Didn't post a screenshot. Just lit a eucalyptus candle, poured a glass of wine, and FaceTimed Jayy.

"Bitch!" was all Jayy had to say.

Myra held up the paper with trembling fingers.

"I passed."

"YOOOOOOOOOO!" Jayy screamed. "Okay, future entrepreneur!"

They stayed on the phone for hours.

Myra lay sprawled on the floor, the bottle almost empty, her cheeks aching from too much laughter.

And for once, she wasn't celebrating a relationship, a birthday, or someone else's dream.

This celebration was hers. Quiet. Sacred. Earned.

Chapter 6
Building My Own Table

With her license in hand, Myra stepped into the next phase of herself.

She joined a prominent firm in Nashville, a sleek downtown office filled with polished agents, designer handbags, and relentless hustle. The lobby smelled like ambition: fresh flowers, leather chairs. The unspoken message was clear: Be sharp, be hungry, or be replaced.

Myra knew this was her shot.

No connections. No head start. Just grit and grace.

Her first weeks were humbling. She shadowed seasoned agents who barely looked her way, took cold calls others ignored, and practiced scripts late at night with Jayy on the other end of the phone pretending to be "Karen from Antioch."

She flubbed a few listings. Forgot a lockbox code once. Missed a follow-up email that cost her a lead.

But she learned. Fast.

Myra read contracts like they were poetry.

She studied neighborhood comps over breakfast.

Watched hours of training videos while deep conditioning her hair.

She said yes to everything: early showings, weekend appointments, out-of-town clients, even the walk-throughs no one else wanted.

And slowly, something shifted. Clients started requesting her. They liked her voice, her warmth, her ability to make people feel safe in the most vulnerable process of their lives.

She remembered birthdays.

Brought lavender-scented candles to new homeowners. Showed up with protein bars and water bottles on moving day. She cared.

And in an industry built on speed and strategy, care stood out. Within six months, Myra wasn't just doing well, she was thriving. Her name was on the leaderboard.

Her phone didn't stop ringing.

Other agents started pulling her aside for advice.

The managing broker, a sharp-eyed woman named Cassandra, called her into the office one Friday afternoon.

Myra thought she'd messed something up.

But instead, Cassandra smiled and handed her a printout. Her name was next to the highest-grossing sale that month.

"Difficult client. Tough price point. You closed it like a pro," Cassandra said, arms crossed but approving. "You've got something special, Myra."

Myra blinked. She wasn't used to being told that outside of a relationship.

"You ever think about running your own show one day?"

The words hit her like a flash forward: her name on a sign, a small boutique office with Black art on the walls and clients hugging her after closing.

A vision. Clear as day.

She smiled slowly, heat blooming in her chest. "I think I just might."

The words stuck with her.

"You ever think about running your own show one day?" Myra had thought about it more than once. But now, with real traction in her career and a name people were beginning to remember, the idea didn't feel so distant. It felt like direction.

Still, she didn't rush it.

She kept her head down. Kept learning. Kept earning.

Every listing taught her something new. Every difficult client, every closing delay, every moment she had to improvise sharpened her, cemented her place in the industry.

And somewhere between showings and signatures, the vision started to take shape.

Every now and then, Nicole resurfaced. A text here.

A reaction to a story there.

A comment under a milestone post:

"Saw you're doing big things. Proud of you." "I miss you. Hope you're doing okay."

Myra never responded.

She wasn't angry anymore, not really. The fire had cooled into ash. But ash still stained, and Myra had no interest in touching something she'd already burned through.

She'd learned that not every wound deserved reopening. Some people don't return because they've changed. They return to see if you have.

Once, Nicole showed up at an open house Myra was hosting.

It was a million-dollar listing: high ceilings, waterfall island, views of the skyline. Myra used to only dream about walking through places like that, much less selling them.

Seeing Nicole standing there, eyes wide, pretending to browse, was jarring. But Myra didn't flinch.

She greeted her the same way she greeted every potential buyer: professionally. Warm, but distant. The mask of a woman who had learned how to separate emotion from execution.

As the event wound down, Nicole lingered by the door.

"You've really made something of yourself," she said, softer than Myra remembered her ever being.

Myra looked her in the eye. Calm. Clear. "I had to."

Nicole nodded. No comeback this time.

She left with nothing but silence behind her. Myra turned the lock and exhaled.

Not because she was shaken, but because she wasn't.

With each passing month, Myra's career grew, and so did her dreams. She started sketching out a plan for her own brokerage. Something small. Personal.

A space where agents felt seen, not squeezed. Where clients weren't just numbers but humans with stories. She wanted her firm to be warm and refined.

Candles burning at the front desk. Music humming low in the background. Coffee table books with Black architects on the covers. A little bowl of peppermints by the entrance, like her grandmother used to keep.

It would take time. And money. And stamina. But she didn't care how long it would take. She was already laying the bricks.

Myra spent her weekends researching LLC structures, attending local networking mixers, and joining online mastermind groups. She started saving aggressively.

No new clothes. No big vacations. Just discipline.

She kept a whiteboard in her kitchen with a handwritten message: "The woman I'm becoming will thank me." But some nights…

When the silence got a little too quiet, and the candle burned a little too low, Myra would scroll.

Old photos.

Moments frozen in joy.

Some she remembered clearly.

Others felt like dreams someone else had lived. And then—

A message. Still unread. Still sitting in her phone like a time capsule from a parallel life.

Luna.

"Hey… been thinking about you. Hope you're okay."

Myra stared at it. Her thumb hovered, not quite touching. She didn't open it.

Not because she didn't care.

But because she cared too much about opening something she wasn't sure she was strong enough to open again.

Luna had always seen her. Not the résumé. Not the image. Her.

Myra had thought of her more than once over the past year, in quiet ways. When a certain scent passed by. When someone laughed just like she used to.

When she wanted to share a win with someone who would understand the cost of it. Luna would be proud of me, she thought. Then she quickly buried it.

Because pride can be a dangerous thing to hope for when distance has turned into silence.

The next morning, Myra arrived at the office earlier than usual.

She hadn't slept much. The wine was long gone, but the memory of Luna's name glowing on her phone lingered. Not in a way that distracted her, more like a song she used to know by heart playing faintly in another room.

She brushed the thought away, locking her focus back on the now. Today mattered. This moment mattered.

She was halfway through reviewing comps when Cassandra, her managing broker, approached her desk with a rare spark in her eyes.

"We've got something," Cassandra said, her voice low but urgent. "Developers on a luxury condo project are looking for an agent to manage the entire portfolio, pre-leasing to close. They want someone sharp. Someone who can carry the weight."

She let the words hang for a beat before adding, "I want it to be you."

Myra sat up straighter. The offer hit like gravity, heavy with meaning, charged with possibility.

"This could be your game changer," Cassandra said. "You nail this, you won't just be the top agent in this firm, you'll be the name they pass around in every closed-door meeting."

Myra's heart thudded, not with fear, but with fire. This was it.

It wasn't just a listing.

It was the first brick of her own empire.

That night, Myra sat at her dining table, the same one she had once used to study for her license, now covered in floorplans, market reports, and sticky notes layered with strategy.

She wasn't intimidated. She was ready.

Everything she had been through, the heartbreak, the healing, the silent nights and quiet rebuilding, had prepared her for this.

This time, she wasn't performing for praise. She was building something real.

For herself.

For the version of her who once doubted she could make it.

And for the woman who would one day run her own show, never forgetting how she got there.

CHAPTER 7
WHERE IT ENDS,
WHERE IT BEGINS

Myra stepped out of the office, her heart still heavy from the conversation with Luna. The weight of unspoken words clung to her like a second skin, making the air feel thick. She needed space, a moment to breathe, but the last thing she wanted right now was to face Jordan.

As she made her way to the front desk, her steps faltered. Jordan stood there, arms crossed, her gaze sharp and unrelenting. The tension between them was palpable, the air charged with all the things they hadn't said and all the things they had.

Myra opened her mouth, but before she could speak, Jordan cut her off.

"Yes, I'm done," Jordan said, her voice sharp. But as she stepped closer, sliding her hands around Myra's hips, her touch was familiar—too familiar. It was reflexive, like muscle memory.

Myra stiffened, instinctively pulling back, but the pull of the past between them was almost magnetic.

"Jordan, stop," Myra said, her voice firm, though the catch in her tone betrayed her conflict.

Jordan leaned in, her lips brushing dangerously close to Myra's, as though trying to reclaim something that had long since unraveled. But Myra turned her head at the last second, avoiding the kiss that threatened to cross a line they had both agreed not to breach again.

"No," Myra said, her voice steady but edged with frustration. "We're not doing this. We've been here before, Jordan, and we both know how it ends." Jordan's face softened, her confidence slipping into something vulnerable. "I made a mistake, Myra," she said, her voice quieter now, almost pleading. "I didn't do enough to make you see that I could be the person you needed. I can be that person."

"You always run when things get too real," Jordan added, her voice barely above a whisper. "You do it with everyone. You're doing it now."

It wasn't just a plea, it was a jab, one designed to plant guilt and hesitation in Myra's chest.

Myra's heart clenched, but she held her ground, stepping away. "No, you didn't," she said, her voice steady despite the sting of her own words. "And it's over. I'm not that person for you anymore. I couldn't even figure out what I wanted.

Jordan's expression flickered with hurt, her voice tight when she responded. "You're pushing me away again, Myra. You're pushing us away."

Myra fought the urge to reach for her, to soothe the pain in Jordan's eyes, but she couldn't, she wouldn't go back. She steadied herself, breathing through the ache in her chest. "We were good at the start," she admitted quietly. "But we're not anymore. And I can't keep pretending otherwise."

Jordan stared at her for a long moment, then held out a piece of paper. "Just sign this," she said, her voice shaky but resolute. "And I'll leave."

Her eyes lingered on Jordan's for a second longer than she meant them to. A flicker of something—grief, nostalgia—

moved through her. Was there a part of her still hoping this could be easier? That maybe the ending didn't have to feel like such a severing? Myra glanced at the letter, what felt like the final piece of their unraveling, and signed it quickly. The act felt heavier than she'd expected, as though she were severing the last thread of what had once been.

As Jordan turned and walked out, her movements stiff with emotion, Myra watched her go, her heart heavy but resolute. The click of the door closing behind her was deafening, the silence that followed suffocating.

"Myra?" Luna's voice broke through the quiet, gentle but firm. Myra turned slowly, leaning against the doorframe, her shoulders sagging with exhaustion.

"Yeah," Myra said, her voice barely above a whisper. "It's done. She's gone."

She walked back into the office, closing the door softly behind her. Luna studied her, her expression a mixture of concern and understanding.

"You don't seem okay," Luna said gently. "You look like you've been through a war out there."

Myra let out a humorless laugh as she sank into the chair opposite Luna. "Maybe I have," she admitted, running a hand through her hair. "Jordan has a way of stirring up old wounds, even the ones I thought I'd healed."

Luna leaned forward, her elbows resting on her knees. "You don't have to tell me everything," she said softly. "But I can tell she still has a hold on you. And that bothers me. Not just because of me, but because you don't deserve to be stuck in that cycle."

Myra met Luna's gaze, her lips parting as though to respond, but no words came. She shook her head, a wry smile tugging at her lips. "You always see right through me, don't you?" Luna shrugged, a small smile playing at her lips. "You're not that hard to read when you're hurting."

The words hit Myra harder than she expected. She dropped her gaze to her hands, her voice soft and reflective. "It's not just about Jordan. It's… everything. My past, the choices I made, the people I hurt, or didn't fight hard enough for." Her voice caught, and she blinked rapidly, pushing back the sting of tears.

Luna reached out, covering Myra's hand with her own. "You're allowed to feel all of that," she said gently. "But you're also allowed to move forward. You don't owe anyone, including Jordan, a version of yourself that you've outgrown."

Myra's head snapped up, her eyes wide. "How do you always know what to say?"

Luna smiled softly. "Practice. And because I've had a long time to think about the kind of things I'd want to say to you if I ever got the chance."

Myra's breath caught, the weight of Luna's words sinking in. "I've missed you," she admitted quietly.

Luna's expression softened, her eyes searching Myra's face. "I missed you too," she said simply, her voice steady but full of emotion.

For the first time in a long time, Myra felt a glimmer of hope, not just for what could be with Luna, but for herself, too. The weight of the past wasn't gone, but for the first time, it felt a little lighter.

Chapter 8
When the Past Still Has a Key

A year had passed since Cassandra handed Myra the deal that changed everything. That portfolio had opened more than doors, it opened Myra's entire future. The commissions stacked fast. The client referrals came without asking. And respect? She didn't have to demand it anymore. She walked into rooms, and people already knew her name.

By the end of that year, Myra had done what she'd once only scribbled on sticky notes: she passed her broker's exam.

Cassandra showed up to the celebration dinner with a bouquet of white calla lilies—Myra's favorite—and a bottle of champagne.

"You were always meant to lead," Cassandra said, raising her glass. "I just saw it early."

Myra choked up for a second before whispering, "Thank you for betting on me."

Myra wasted no time.

She found a medium commercial space tucked between a coffee shop and a yoga studio: just enough character, just enough parking. She signed the lease with a shaky hand and a steady heart.

The build-out took months. The vision? Crystal clear.

She recruited two seasoned agents and one hungry rookie who reminded Myra of herself.

She painted the walls a warm cream, lit incense before every morning meeting, and placed her logo—sharp and feminine—gleaming in gold on the front door.

Myra was now Broker Myra. And it felt right.

A few months into running her firm, the opportunity came like a whisper.

A well-known Nashville musician, Jaxon Creed, needed help finding an estate on the outskirts of town. Discretion and trust were non-negotiable. Myra came recommended by an old client who called her "the real estate fairy godmother."

The musician's team reached out, and a date was set to tour a five-bedroom, two-story home nestled on a private lot lined with oaks.

Myra arrived early, every detail in place: water bottles chilled, printed packets ready, a fresh touch of perfume behind her ears.

She was mid-sentence, pointing out the original hardwood flooring in the living room, when she felt it.

Energy.

Not loud. Not jarring. Just… unmistakable. She looked up.

Leaning against the far wall, arms crossed, stood a woman she hadn't noticed before. Tall. Calm.

Piercing hazel eyes.

A gaze that cut straight through pretense and hit her like a forgotten song. Myra paused.

Words tripped over each other on her tongue. Her chest fluttered in a way that had nothing to do with nerves.

"Jordan," the client's wife said, motioning toward her. "Our daughter. She'll be helping us decide."

Myra nodded politely, but her heart hadn't caught up.

Jordan tilted her head slightly, studying Myra like she was reading something on her soul. Feeling a bit flustered, Myra cleared her throat and refocused on the tour.

Still, with every room they walked through, she felt Jordan's eyes lingering. Not in a way that demanded attention, but in a way that held it.

Jordan's presence wasn't just about how she looked, though that alone could turn heads. There was a calm confidence in the way she stood, the slight tilt of her head, the quiet pull in her energy. It was disarming—familiar in a way Myra couldn't explain.

It wasn't Nicole.

It wasn't anything Myra had ever had.

But it felt like something she'd been looking for without knowing it.

Jordan's energy carried a softness edged with fire, a balance Myra hadn't seen in anyone since before. It unsettled her, but not in a way that made her shrink. Instead, it made her want to stand taller.

Myra kept her tone light and professional, but the space between them buzzed. Jordan didn't try to interrupt the tour or dominate the conversation. She just asked questions, made sharp observations, and listened in a way most people didn't.

Then her mother's phone rang, pulling her out of the moment. She stepped into another room to take the call, leaving Myra and Jordan alone in the den.

"So," Jordan began, her voice low and smooth, "I noticed there's a ring on your finger. Are you married?" Myra glanced down at her hand, suddenly aware of the gold band still resting on her finger. A remnant of her past with Nicole. She wore it more out of habit than meaning now, the absence of it making her finger feel strangely naked.

"No," Myra said quietly. "It's just a ring from something that didn't work out."

Jordan nodded slowly, her expression softening. "I can relate. I was engaged once, but things just fell apart."

The air between them was thick and charged, almost sacred. The words were simple, but they unlocked something deeper, something both of them recognized but couldn't quite name.

As they walked through the last few rooms of the house, Myra found herself slowing down. Not for the sake of the showing, but for the sake of presence. For the first time in a long time, she wanted someone to stay just a little bit longer.

At the end of the tour, Jordan's mother thanked Myra for her time, her tone warm and decisive. "This might be the one," she said, glancing at her daughter before looking back to Myra. "We'll be in touch soon."

Myra nodded, offering a gracious smile. Another successful showing. Another step forward.

But just as they were heading out the front door, Jordan lingered.

She turned back, her voice soft but confident. "Do you want to grab a drink sometime?"

Myra blinked, caught off guard by the directness. Her body flushed with warmth, and she studied Jordan's expression for a beat—casual, but hopeful. There was no pressure in her tone, just an openness. An invitation.

Myra hadn't expected this. She hadn't even realized she'd been hoping for it.

After a brief pause, she smirked. "Yeah. I do."

Jordan's smile deepened, the corners of her eyes crinkling. "How about tonight?"

Myra hesitated, instinctively thinking about her quiet rituals: her wine, her playlists, the safety of solitude she had grown to rely on. But then she remembered the way Jordan had watched her earlier, the calm weight of her presence, the way her words seemed to reach past the surface.

She exhaled slowly. "Tonight works."

They exchanged numbers, fingers grazing slightly as Myra handed her phone over. When Jordan walked away, Myra stood in the doorway for a moment, watching her go.

For the first time in what felt like years, something stirred in her—light, unexpected, and alive.

She closed the door gently behind her, her heart fluttering in a way she hadn't allowed in a long, long time.

That night, Myra met Jordan at a quiet bar tucked away on the edge of the city. Dim lights, soft music, and the hum of low conversation wrapped the place in a calm she hadn't realized she needed. Jordan was already at the table, a half-smile tugging at her lips when she saw Myra walk in.

Over drinks, the conversation was easy. Effortless, even. They swapped stories, teased each other playfully, and fell into laughter that felt honest. Jordan had a way of drawing Myra out without pushing. Her charm ran deeper than smooth words—it lived in her curiosity, in the way she actually listened, in the steadiness of her gaze.

Still, there was something more. A quiet edge. Jordan spoke with poise, but Myra could tell there were things beneath the surface. Things she hadn't said yet.

As the night wound down, they stepped out into the cool air. Across the street, a small park sat under the soft glow of streetlamps.

Jordan paused, pulling a blunt from her purse and raising a brow.

"Nightcap walk?"

Myra hesitated for a moment. She didn't usually say yes to things like this. But tonight already felt different. She shrugged, a smirk forming. "Sure. Why not?"

They wandered the park's winding paths, the scent of weed mingling with fresh-cut grass and summer air. The moon cast shadows across the trail, and for a while, they just walked in silence.

Then Jordan passed the blunt to Myra, and something shifted. Maybe it was the setting, or the haze settling between them, but Myra felt her guard begin to loosen.

She started talking. Not just the surface-level stuff, but the real things. The kind she didn't usually say out loud. Her voice was soft but steady as she spoke about her past: the relationships that broke her open, the ways she'd had to rebuild herself, her fears of trusting too easily, and what it meant to start over again when everything she thought she wanted had collapsed.

Jordan didn't interrupt. She just listened, nodding occasionally, her expression unreadable but warm.

Myra hadn't known what to expect from the night. Maybe a drink, maybe a laugh. Certainly not this—not the feeling of being seen without having to explain herself. And as they sat on a park bench beneath the stars, something inside her quietly lightened.

It wasn't love. Not yet. But it was something.

At one point, it truly felt like Jordan understood her. Understood everything Myra had carried through the years.

"You ever feel like some people come into your life for a reason?" Jordan asked, her voice quieter now, more serious.

Myra nodded, caught off guard by the weight of the question. "Yeah," she said softly. "Like they've been there before somehow. Like you're supposed to meet them."

Jordan smiled faintly. "I feel that right now. With you."

She reached out, brushing her fingers lightly down Myra's wrist. The touch wasn't demanding. It was delicate, intentional.

And Myra felt it—that sensation again, the one that whispered she had met Jordan long before this moment, in some other place, in some other life. It was spiritual. Familiar. Jordan stirred something in her, bringing emotions to the surface that Myra thought she had buried too deep to be touched: grief, longing, hope.

The intensity of it frightened Myra.

But she didn't want to back away. Not from this. Not from someone who made her feel seen in a way that didn't require her to shrink.

"Okay," Myra said, barely above a whisper. "I'm willing to explore this attraction with you."

Jordan's smile deepened, her eyes bright with something soft and wild. "Good, because I want to explore it too."

Things moved quickly after that. Their relationship began to unfold in a blur of late-night conversations, spontaneous meetups, and shared silences that said more than words ever could.

To Myra, it still felt more like a friendship—one tangled in flirtation and tension, but not grounded in the emotional intimacy she was used to.

Jordan's charm was effortless, magnetic. But sometimes it felt too polished, too practiced. Myra couldn't help but wonder if every sweet word was real or just perfectly timed.

Their connection was undeniable, but it lacked the emotional depth she craved. Still, Myra stayed. Because for the first time in a long time, someone made her feel alive. And sometimes, that was enough.

As they grew closer, Jordan slowly pulled back the velvet curtain of her world. Myra met her family's glossy legacy of wealth and reputation with a quiet sense of awe and unease. Everything had been handed to Jordan, yet she wanted to carve her own name into the world. She wasn't content to coast on generational comfort.

Jordan had been developing a talk show for a while, and she spoke about it with such clarity and confidence that Myra couldn't help but be impressed. Jordan wanted success on her own terms, and Myra admired that.

Still, their lives couldn't have been more different. Myra's journey had been built on survival—scraping by, failing forward, rebuilding brick by brick. She had no soft landing, no wealthy safety net to fall into. But Jordan's spark was infectious. There was something beautiful about her confidence. It made Myra want to dream a little bolder, too.

As their relationship deepened, Myra found herself falling for the way Jordan laughed with her whole face, the way she studied Myra's expressions, the way she made her feel chosen. But beneath the surface, a quiet unease remained.

Nicole still haunted the edges of Myra's heart.

Myra was in the middle of a board meeting, listening to projections and next-quarter goals, when her phone buzzed. She glanced at it quickly under the table.

Nicole: *My car is totaled. I have no way to get to work. Can I use one of yours? Please.*

Myra's stomach tightened. The name alone reopened something she had worked hard to seal shut. She hesitated before responding.

Myra: *Nicole, this isn't a good idea.*

Nicole: *I don't have anyone else, Myra. I wouldn't ask if it wasn't serious.*

Please.

Myra sighed quietly, that old, familiar guilt bubbling up again— the part of her that always wanted to be helpful, needed to be needed.

Myra: *Fine. Just be careful, okay? Pick it up after 7.*

Nicole: *Thank you, Myra. I owe you one.*

The conversation left a sour taste in her mouth. Her past with Nicole was like a ghost she couldn't quite exorcise. No matter how far she ran, it always knew how to find her.

Later that night, Jordan texted her. Myra tried to keep the conversation light, but something in her tone must have shifted.

Jordan: *You okay? You seem… off.*

Myra: *I'm fine. Just a lot on my mind.*

Jordan: *Myra. I know you better than that. Spill.*

She hesitated, then typed.

Myra: *Nicole texted me. She's having car trouble. I told her she could borrow one of mine.*

A pause.

Jordan: *Wow… Do you still love her?*

Myra stared at the question. Her thumb hovered over the keyboard. What was the truth? What did she owe herself?

Myra: *I care about her. But no, I'm not in love with her anymore. I fell out of love when I realized I wasn't her priority.*

Jordan: *It's okay to care, Myra. But don't let her pull you back into something that's not healthy.*

Myra: *I know. You're right. I need to focus on moving forward.*

Jordan: *Good. Because you deserve that.*

Myra sat back against her pillows, the phone warm in her hand. She thought about all the times she had prioritized others over herself—the relationships she poured into, hoping to be enough. And now, here she was, finally creating a life on her own terms.

But even as she tried to move forward, the past had a way of lingering.

She glanced at the keys she had set aside for Nicole. Maybe this was the last time. Maybe letting go didn't always look like slamming the door shut, it could be quiet—a boundary drawn softly but firmly.

Myra turned off the light. Tomorrow would come, and with it, another opportunity to keep choosing herself.

CHAPTER 9
TWO FISH IN THE SAME OCEAN

Myra and Jordan discovered they shared the same zodiac sign, Pisces.

"We're like two sides of the same coin," Jordan joked one evening as they sipped red wine on the couch, feet tangled beneath a throw blanket. "You're the grounded Pisces. I'm the impulsive one."

Myra smirked, setting her glass down. "You mean I clean up your chaos."

Jordan grinned. "Exactly."

Their birthdays were just days apart in late February. Myra hadn't celebrated hers in years, at least not in a way that felt intentional. Most came and went with little more than a text or a dinner that never quite landed. So when Jordan surprised her with a trip to Jamaica, Myra was stunned.

"You're serious?"

Jordan handed her the itinerary with a smug smile. "Flights. Hotel. I even cleared your calendar."

Myra blinked. "How?"

"Called your assistant. She's a gem, by the way."

Myra laughed despite herself. "You're ridiculous." "And you're coming."

From the moment they landed in Montego Bay, Myra felt the tension she carried begin to melt. The thick air, fragrant with salt and spices, wrapped around her like a warm shawl. Jordan moved through the island as if it were stitched into her bones, knowing exactly where to eat, which beaches to visit, which backroads led to the most breathtaking views.

Myra followed her lead. She let go.

On their second night, they walked the beach barefoot under a sky blanketed with stars. The ocean whispered softly at their feet, and music from a nearby bonfire pulsed gently in the background.

"I used to come here every summer," Jordan said, eyes fixed on the water. "With my dad. This place... it's in me."

Myra didn't ask questions. She just listened. She was learning that with Jordan, sometimes the silences said more than the stories.

The next day, they rode scooters along the coast, stopping for foil-wrapped jerk chicken and roadside coconuts. Jordan drove like she had no fear. Myra held on, her laugh catching in the wind, the moment too pure to second-guess.

That night, Jordan led her to a quiet cove, just the two of them and the hush of the tide. They waded into the moonlit water until it reached their waists, then drifted in silence.

Myra tilted her head toward the sky. "It's peaceful here."

Jordan floated beside her, arms stretched wide. "It's honest. That's what I love about it."

Back at their suite, with skin still damp and hair clinging to their necks, Jordan reached into her bag and pulled out a small box. Inside was a delicate gold necklace with a Pisces charm.

Myra blinked. "You didn't have to..."

Jordan clasped it behind her neck. "I wanted to. You wear your strength like armor, but I see what's underneath."

Myra looked at herself in the mirror, fingers grazing the charm. She hadn't expected this trip to unravel her the way it did, to feel seen in a way that wasn't about saving someone, fixing something, or proving her worth.

During the trip, Jordan invited Myra to meet an old friend, Rhailyn.

They met at a seaside café tucked beneath swaying palms, the ocean just a few steps away. Rhailyn was stunning: bronzed skin that caught the sun, long thick curls, and a smile that immediately made Myra feel welcome. But it was the unspoken familiarity between Rhailyn and Jordan that Myra couldn't ignore.

There was an ease to their conversation, the kind that only came with time and shared history. Inside jokes. Lingering glances. That subtle electricity Myra recognized all too well. Still, she played it cool, laughing along and asking questions, trying not to overanalyze every look between them.

When she excused herself to the restroom, something tensed between Jordan and Rhailyn.

Rhailyn leaned back in her chair, her sharp eyes studying Jordan with a mix of nostalgia and curiosity.

"She seems sweet," she said lightly, though her tone was probing.

Jordan shrugged, a small smile playing on her lips. "She is. Complicated, though. But who isn't?"

Rhailyn tilted her head, letting her curls fall over one shoulder.

"You've always been drawn to complicated. Remember us?"

Jordan laughed softly, the sound laced with both warmth and hesitation. "How could I forget? You were the definition of complicated."

Rhailyn smirked but didn't let up. "So, what's her deal? She's gorgeous, obviously. But I can tell there's more going on."

Jordan sighed, swirling her drink. "She's got this past, this ex who's still lingering. It's messy. And sometimes I wonder if she's really ready to move on, or if I'm just a distraction."

Rhailyn's brow furrowed. "Do you feel like that? Like she's using you to forget someone else?"

Jordan paused. "I don't think it's intentional. I see the way she looks at me. There's something real there. But I also see the hesitation, like part of her is still holding back."

Rhailyn leaned forward, resting her elbows on the table. "You've always had a soft spot for the ones who don't know what they want."

Jordan's gaze snapped to Rhailyn's, a flicker of defiance in her eyes. "It's not like that with Myra. She's different. There's something about her, like I've known her forever, even though we've just met. I can't explain it, but it feels right."

Rhailyn's expression softened. "Sounds like you're hooked."

Jordan chuckled. "Maybe I am. But it's not just about her, it's about me too. I'm not sure if I'm ready for something serious either."

Rhailyn raised an eyebrow. "So you're both dancing around it? Let me guess, you haven't had the 'what are we' talk yet?"

Jordan leaned back and exhaled sharply. "Not exactly. We're in this undefined space. We're not exclusive, but it's more than casual. It's just..."

"Confusing," Rhailyn finished for her, smirking. Jordan gave a faint smile. "Yeah. Confusing."

Rhailyn reached across the table and rested a hand on Jordan's. "Look, when you care, you give everything, even when you're not sure where it's headed. But you can't keep pouring yourself into something if you're not both ready. You'll burn out."

Jordan looked down at their hands. "I know. It's just hard. Myra feels different, but I don't know if I should push or let it unfold naturally."

Rhailyn's voice dropped to something softer. "Do you remember how it felt when we were together? How everything seemed so intense, like it was all or nothing?"

Jordan's breath caught. "Of course I remember."

"That's what you're chasing with Myra, isn't it?" Rhailyn asked. "That feeling of connection, of being fully seen. But sometimes that kind of connection burns too bright. Be careful with her, and with yourself."

Jordan swallowed, her voice low. "I'm trying. But it's not just about the connection. It's about her. There's something about her that makes me want to stay, even when it's messy."

Rhailyn nodded slowly. "Then stay. But make sure she's ready to let you in. You can't build something real if one of you is still living in the past."

The bathroom door creaked open, and Myra returned to the table, sliding into the seat beside Jordan and glancing between the two women.

"So," she said lightly, though her eyes lingered on Jordan a beat too long. "What were you two talking about?"

Jordan opened her mouth to respond, but not before Myra caught a quick look exchanged between her and Rhailyn. It wasn't flirtatious, at least not in the traditional sense. It felt more like a flicker of unspoken understanding, something familiar that didn't need to be said aloud. Still, it tugged at something deep in Myra's stomach, a subtle unease she couldn't quite name.

Jordan smiled, her tone breezy. "Just catching up. Rhailyn was filling me in on life here in Jamaica."

Rhailyn's gaze didn't waver. She let out a soft laugh, her voice smooth. "And reminding her not to get in over her head."

Myra raised an eyebrow. There was something beneath the surface—too light to confront, but heavy enough to notice. She kept her voice playful, masking the edge. "Well, I hope she's listening."

Jordan slipped an arm around Myra's shoulders, leaning in close, her smile warm. "I always listen," she said. "Even if I don't always follow advice."

The days that followed blurred into a gentle rhythm: golden sunsets, easy laughter, and moments that made Myra question if this was just a getaway or the start of something real.

One afternoon, they wandered through a bustling craft market. Myra's eyes lit up at every stall: woven baskets, vibrant paintings, spices in glass jars. Jordan trailed behind her, occasionally stepping in with charm and practiced ease to negotiate a lower price.

"You act like you've done this a hundred times," Myra said, holding up a necklace of tiny, polished shells.

"I have," Jordan replied, her smirk lazy. "But not like this. Not with you."

The look in her eyes made Myra's cheeks flush, her chest tightening with a feeling she hadn't expected to find here.

At night, they sat barefoot in the sand, waves crashing in the distance as they traded stories like secrets. Myra opened up in a way she hadn't with anyone in a long time: about childhood dreams, about life's detours, about the parts of herself she usually kept tucked away.

Jordan listened quietly, her gaze on the horizon.

"You know," she said after a while, "being with you feels… familiar."

Myra looked over. "Familiar how?"

Jordan took a moment, her voice softer now. "Like we've met before. Not just in this life."

Myra smiled, surprised by the way those words sank into her.

"I've felt that too."

Jordan nodded. "It's strange, right? That something can feel this real so fast?"

Myra didn't answer. She reached down and let her fingers drag through the sand, grounding herself in the present.

The next morning, Jordan surprised her with horseback riding along the beach. Myra had never done it before, and it showed— her laughter echoed each time her horse shifted unexpectedly. But as they rode together, the wind on their skin and the ocean at their side, Myra felt a calm she hadn't known she needed.

"I could stay here forever," Myra said, glancing at Jordan, who rode beside her with ease.

That night, back at the villa, the windows were open and the ocean breeze drifted in, warm and fragrant with salt and hibiscus. The sound of waves crashing just beyond the porch blended with the low hum of music playing in the background.

Myra stood barefoot by the sliding doors, looking out at the moonlit sea. Her skin still held the sun's warmth, her hair tousled from the ride.

Jordan came up behind her, wrapping her arms gently around Myra's waist, pressing her cheek to her shoulder. "You really meant it," Jordan whispered. "About staying."

Myra leaned back into her, eyes still on the water. "For a moment, it felt like we were outside of time."

Jordan turned her slowly, hands lingering at Myra's hips. Their eyes met in the soft glow of the villa lights, something unspoken crackling between them. Jordan's fingers brushed Myra's cheek, then her jawline, before resting at the base of her neck.

"You feel like a dream," Jordan murmured.

Myra didn't reply. She closed the distance between them.

Their lips met, slow at first, as if testing the depth of what had been building—then deeper. The kind of kiss that made Myra forget where she was. Jordan's hands slipped beneath the hem of Myra's tank top, thumbs tracing the curve of her waist.

They moved toward the bed with a shared breath, laughter flickering between kisses, clothes forgotten piece by piece. It wasn't rushed. It was reverent.

Jordan touched Myra like she was something precious. Myra gave in like she had finally stopped holding her breath.

Outside, the waves crashed and the wind carried the scent of night jasmine. Inside, time fell away.

"We could make a life here. You, me, and the horses," Jordan said.

Myra laughed, the sound soft and full. "You'd be bored in a week."

Jordan shrugged, still smiling as her eyes lingered on Myra.

"Maybe. But for now, it's a nice thought."

Myra looked out at the sea, the sun beginning to dip low against the horizon and casting the sky in amber. The breeze tousled her curls, and Jordan reached out to tuck a strand behind her ear.

"It really is," Myra whispered, not entirely sure if she meant the moment or the possibility of something more.

For a while, they just sat there, side by side, in no rush to return to the real world.

Chapter 10
Situational Magic The Plane Ride Home Was Silent.

Myra stared out the window, the clouds beneath them like soft lies cushioning a hard truth: Jamaica was over. The golden sunsets, the warmth of Jordan's touch, the way it all felt like maybe, just maybe, something real was forming—it was already fading behind them.

Jordan sat beside her, unusually quiet. Her charm, always effortless, was dialed down to something Myra couldn't read.

When Myra finally asked, "What's on your mind?" Jordan offered a vague smile. "Just thinking about what's next."

Next. The word lingered like a thread Myra couldn't quite pull.

At baggage claim, Jordan kissed her cheek and murmured, "I'll call you later," but the way her eyes didn't quite meet Myra's said more than she let on.

Back in her apartment, the silence was immediate and jarring. Myra leaned against the door, the cool air biting against her skin as if to remind her this was reality now. Not island nights and moonlit confessions, just bills, business, and figuring out if what she felt was real or just situational magic.

The next morning, Myra walked into her brokerage office with her game face on. The floor-to-ceiling windows flooded the room with light, but everything felt dimmer. Jamaica was a dream she wasn't ready to wake from.

Then she saw the empty front desk. A sticky note on the monitor read:

Myra, I'm sorry. I've taken another job. I couldn't wait for things to stabilize. Wishing you the best. Lucy—her assistant, her anchor—was gone.

Myra crumpled the note in her hand. No time to panic. Not now. Not today.

Her inbox was chaos: clients, invoices, deals that still hadn't closed. And then, a call that pulled her back to center.

"Ms. Edwards, this is Mr. Greene. Are we still on for two o'clock?"

"Yes," she said without hesitation, her voice steady. "I'll see you then."

When the meeting ended, Myra felt something rare: hope. He was interested. Maybe she could do this after all.

But that confidence faltered as she caught herself checking her phone for a text that wasn't there.

Jordan was radio silent.

By six, the office was dark again. Myra sat at her desk, staring at the city lights. She'd made it through day one without Lucy. Without Jordan. Without answers. Starting over was never easy, but this was hers.

A few weeks passed, and the brokerage began to buzz with new energy. She'd hired five agents. Deals were closing. But the missing assistant left her overextended, pulled in every direction.

Then, a text lit up her screen:

Thinking of stopping by your office later. You cool with that?
–J

Her heart fluttered. She hated that it still did.

"Of course," she typed, too casually.

Jordan arrived an hour later, holding a Starbucks cup like a peace offering.

"Look at you," she teased, eyeing Myra's frazzled state. "You're two emails away from snapping."

Myra smirked, taking the drink. "Careful, you'll make me expect this."

"Wouldn't dream of spoiling you," Jordan said, but her gaze lingered longer than it should have, carrying something heavier than the joke.

Myra gave a soft laugh, glancing at the stack of papers beside her. "If you really wanted to help, you'd sit at that empty desk out front and start sorting through these contracts."

Jordan leaned against the counter, sipping her own drink. "Don't tempt me."

Myra raised a brow. "I'm serious."

Jordan studied her for a moment, then straightened. "So am I."

Myra blinked. "Wait, you'd actually do it?"

Jordan shrugged, casual but not careless. "I've got time. You clearly don't. And watching you unravel one to-do list at a time isn't exactly entertaining."

Myra hesitated. "Jordan, this is a business. My business. It's not just coffee runs and calendar invites."

"Good thing I'm not just a pretty face," she said, flashing a grin. "Come on, Myra. Let me help. Temporary. Until you find someone."

Myra wanted to protest, to list off all the reasons this was a bad idea—boundaries, emotions, blurred lines—but instead, she just said, "You'd really do that?"

Jordan's expression softened. "Yeah. I would."

Myra exhaled slowly. "Fine. But no special treatment. You mess up, I'm writing you up like anyone else."

Jordan laughed. "Can't wait to see your HR file."

By the end of the week, Jordan was at the front desk organizing contracts, answering phones, and somehow managing to make the place feel like it was running smoother than ever.

Not as a girlfriend.

Not even really as a friend. Just her temporary assistant.

And somehow, that was more dangerous than anything they'd shared in Jamaica. Jordan was sharp, efficient, and natural with people. She fit. Too well.

Their workdays began to blur: quiet touches, lingering looks, flirtation that buzzed just beneath their professionalism. It was a dance, subtle and slow, with a rhythm neither dared name. Boundaries existed in theory, but in practice they bent in all the familiar ways.

They were careful not to let the other agents notice. No inside jokes in meetings, no accidental glances that lasted too long. Whatever this was, if it was anything, they kept it tucked between late nights and private silences.

Late one night, long after the others had gone, Jordan popped her head into Myra's office.

"You know it's almost ten, right?"

Myra didn't look up. "So?"

Jordan crossed the room, closed the laptop, and gave her a look that stilled everything. "You need to go home."

Myra nodded, caught in the softness of Jordan's eyes. It wasn't concern. It was something deeper. Something she wasn't sure she could afford to believe in.

They walked out together, silence thick between them. Just before they parted, Myra said, "Thanks. For everything."

Jordan's voice was light, but her eyes weren't. "Just don't expect me to carry you forever."

Myra laughed, but it caught in her throat. The tension snapped a few nights later.

They were alone again, the office cloaked in after-hours silence, lit only by the city's glow spilling through the windows. The hum of the air conditioner was steady, but the air between them pulsed with something hotter, heavier.

"You need a break," Jordan said, voice low, eyes fixed on Myra like she was the only thing in the room worth looking at.

Myra didn't look up from her laptop. "I can't afford one."

Jordan stepped closer, her tone dipping into something that made Myra's breath catch. "Maybe you don't need time off. Maybe you just need… a release."

Myra finally met her gaze. Everything in her tightened. The stare wasn't playful. It was loaded.

Jordan didn't wait.

She crossed the remaining space in three measured steps, took Myra's face in her hands, and kissed her like she'd been holding it in for months, like she was starving and Myra was the only thing that could feed the hunger.

It was fast and slow all at once. Fingers tangled in hair, breath caught between lips, months of flirtation unraveling in seconds. Myra's back hit the desk, papers scattering like they didn't matter—and in that moment, they didn't. Only this did.

When they finally pulled apart, both breathless and flushed, neither of them said a word. Myra didn't ask what it meant. She wasn't sure she wanted to hear the answer.

And the next day, Jordan didn't mention it. She never did.

Chapter 11
The Closure That Was Never Yours to Give

The quiet hum of the city filled Myra's condo as she and Jordan sat on the couch, the remnants of their takeout scattered across the coffee table. The conversation had ebbed into a comfortable silence, Jordan reclining against the cushions while Myra leaned forward, her fingers absently swirling the wine in her glass. Moments like this felt almost too easy, like the chaos of their lives was temporarily suspended.

Jordan glanced at Myra, a smirk tugging at her lips. "You're actually relaxing. I'm impressed."

Myra laughed softly, shaking her head. "Don't get used to it. This is a rare occurrence."

"Well," Jordan said, leaning closer, her voice dropping into something softer, "you should make it less rare. You deserve to have moments like this." look dry.

Myra felt the weight of Jordan's words settle over her, the sincerity in her tone tugging at something deep inside. Jordan was in one of her softest moods, shoulders relaxed, gaze warm— the kind of night that made it hard to keep walls up.

Another night. Takeout on Myra's couch. The room dim except for the glow of the city outside. Myra almost said, what are we doing? But instead, she said, "This feels dangerous."

Jordan didn't flinch. Her answer came easy: "Life's messy. Doesn't mean it's not worth it."

Myra smiled at that, but the truth sat heavy in her chest. How long could she keep risking everything for someone who never stayed long enough to answer?

She was about to respond when a knock at the door shattered the stillness. Myra frowned, setting her glass down. "Who could that be?"

Jordan straightened, her playful expression giving way to curiosity. "Expecting anyone?" "No." Myra stood, brushing her hands against her jeans as she walked to the door. When she opened it, her breath caught in her throat.

There, standing in the hallway with an air of casual confidence, was Nicole. She held a set of car keys in her hand, her expression unreadable as her eyes flickered to Myra's startled face.

"Hey," Nicole said, her tone deceptively light. "Thought I'd drop these off. Thanks for letting me borrow your car while mine was in the shop."

Myra froze, her chest tightening. "You didn't have to come all the way here."

Nicole shrugged, leaning against the doorframe like she belonged there. "I figured it was time. Besides, I wanted to catch up. You've been… busy."

Before Myra could respond, Jordan appeared behind her, leaning casually against the wall. "She's got company," Jordan said, her tone neutral but her presence impossible to ignore.

Nicole's gaze shifted to Jordan, her smirk faltering for a split second. Her eyes narrowed, taking in the scene—the casual intimacy of Jordan's stance, the faint buzz of conversation that had lingered in the air when she arrived.

"Well," Nicole said, her voice sharper now. "I didn't realize you'd moved on so quickly."

Myra's jaw tightened, her tone measured as she stepped forward. "Nicole, I appreciate you dropping the keys off, but this isn't the time."

Nicole raised an eyebrow, her smirk returning but tinged with something colder. "Right. Wouldn't want to interrupt."

Jordan's expression stayed neutral, but Myra could feel the tension radiating from her. "It's fine," Jordan said evenly, moving back toward the living room. "I'll let you handle this."

Myra exhaled, stepping out into the hallway and closing the door slightly behind her. "What are you doing here, Nicole?" Nicole's expression softened, a flicker of vulnerability crossing her face. "I just… thought I'd see how you're doing. I mean, you lend me your car and then leave for Jamaica without saying much. It's like you're trying to erase everything we had."

Myra crossed her arms, keeping her voice steady. "I lent you the car because you needed it, not as an invitation to dig up the past. We're done, Nicole. You know that."

Nicole's jaw tightened, and for a moment, she looked like she might argue. But then she shook her head, holding out the keys. "Fine. I just thought maybe you'd want to talk. Guess I was wrong."

"There's nothing left to talk about. I'm glad your car's fixed, but this—whatever you're trying to do—it's not going to work."

Nicole's gaze lingered on Myra for a long moment before she stepped back, the mask of confidence slipping slightly. "Let's not pretend you're done with me. You're just pretending better than usual."

Myra didn't flinch. She laughed, sharp and humorless, hollow. "Wow. You really believe that, don't you?"

Nicole raised an eyebrow, but Myra didn't wait. The dam had broken.

"You really think I'm pretending? You think I'm playing some game where you're still the prize? Nicole, you weren't even the bare minimum. You drained me. You lied, disappeared, reappeared, gave just enough to keep me holding on, and when I finally stopped chasing you, you took it personal. You think my healing is about you?"

Myra stepped forward, her voice rising, steady and venom-laced with truth.

"You don't get to show up here with your smug little smirk and act like you're checking on me. You're not here for closure, you're here for control. Because for the first time, you're not the center of my life, and that bruises your ego."

Nicole's jaw tensed, but Myra kept going.

"You played me. Over and over. And I let you—because I loved you. I saw your potential, not your reality. I made excuses for your silence, your coldness, your mess. I watered a dead thing and blamed myself when it didn't grow. And now, after everything, you think you can pop up, drop off some keys like you're doing me a favor, and slide back into my peace?"

Nicole's smile twitched, cold and cutting. "You act like I ruined you."

Myra's eyes burned. "No. You didn't ruin me. I let myself shrink for you. I ignored red flags like they were roses. I twisted myself into someone you could love, someone small enough to make you feel big. And you still left me empty."

Nicole crossed her arms, defensive. "I never asked you to do all that."

"And that's exactly the problem," Myra snapped. "You never asked. You just took. You let me pour into you and never once thought about what it cost me."

She took a breath, chest heaving, voice cracking but never breaking.

"You don't get to make me feel guilty for surviving you. For finally choosing me. For not answering your calls or texts. For not chasing you like I used to. You had access to me, and you wasted it."

Nicole opened her mouth to speak again, but Myra was already stepping back.

"You don't belong here. Not in this version of me and not in this future I'm building without you."

She snatched the keys from Nicole's hand, not gently. "Goodbye, Nicole. For real this time."

For the first time since Myra opened the door, Nicole didn't have anything to say. Her mouth closed, her jaw flexed, but no words came. Just silence. And a flash of something almost human in her eyes. Regret, maybe. Or the dawning realization that Myra meant every word.

Myra didn't wait to see what Nicole would do next. She turned, walked back inside, and shut the door behind her slowly, firmly, like sealing off a chapter. No more unfinished conversations. No more silent suffering.

Jordan looked up from the couch, eyebrows slightly raised. She didn't ask what happened.

Myra didn't offer it.

She just stood for a moment, letting the weight of the last few minutes settle into her chest, then exhaled slowly, long, full of years of holding her tongue.

"So that was Nicole," Jordan said. Her jaw ticked for a fraction of a second, barely noticeable unless you were looking for it. She kept her voice even, but her arms remained crossed, like she was still deciding how she felt about all of it.

After Nicole left, the apartment felt heavy, as though her presence had left an invisible weight in the air. Myra leaned against the closed door for a moment, her breath steady but shallow, trying to collect her thoughts. The keys sat in her hand, cool against her palm, and for some reason, they felt heavier than they should.

When she turned around, Jordan was watching her, her expression carefully neutral but her arms still crossed, as though bracing for something.

"You okay?" Jordan asked, her voice quiet but laced with curiosity.

Myra nodded, though her chest felt tight. "Yeah. Just… old ghosts."

Jordan uncrossed her arms and leaned against the wall, her casual posture a stark contrast to the tension still radiating from Myra. "She doesn't look like the kind of ghost that's ready to let go."

Myra exhaled deeply, walking over to the counter and placing the keys down with more force than necessary. "She's not," she admitted. "But that's not my problem anymore."

Jordan pushed off the wall, following her. "You sure? Because she seems to think it is."

Myra met Jordan's gaze, her lips pressing into a thin line. "It's not," she said firmly. "It hasn't been for a long time. Nicole… she's always been good at finding ways to linger, but I've moved on."

Jordan tilted her head, studying Myra's face. "Good. Because you deserve better than someone who can't respect your boundaries."

Myra looked down, a faint smile tugging at the corners of her mouth. "Thanks," she murmured. "I know that. Now."

Jordan didn't press further, instead shifting the conversation with her usual ease. "So," she said, nudging Myra lightly with her shoulder, "want me to help you throw those keys off the balcony? Symbolic gesture and all."

Myra laughed despite herself, the sound breaking the tension in the room. "Tempting. But I think I'll just put them in a drawer and forget they exist for a while."

She moved toward the side table by the couch, opening the drawer and placing the keys inside. Her hand hovered for a second before she closed it. A flicker of something—grief, maybe, or guilt—brushed her ribs. She hated that it was still there, still lingering. But she shut the drawer anyway.

As it clicked shut, she felt something unexpected: a small sense of relief. It wasn't just about the keys. It was about putting something behind her, one small step at a time.

Jordan flopped onto the couch, patting the spot next to her. "Come on," she said. "I've got a much better distraction for you than Nicole and her borrowed car drama."

Myra raised an eyebrow, smirking as she sat down. "Oh? And what's that?"

Jordan grinned, picking up the remote. "I discovered this terrible real estate reality show while you were working the other day. It's bad—like, really bad. But I figure we can make fun of it together."

Myra shook her head, laughing softly as she leaned into the cushions. "You're ridiculous, you know that?"

Jordan gave her a mock-serious look. "Ridiculous or brilliant? The line is thinner than you think."

As the show started, Myra felt herself relax for the first time since Nicole had knocked on her door. She glanced at Jordan, who was already critiquing the show's overly dramatic narration, and let herself enjoy the moment.

Chapter 12
I'm Still Figuring It Out

The late afternoon sun spilled across Myra's office, casting long shadows over the desk as if trying to reveal what had been hidden between them. Jordan leaned against the edge, scrolling through listings on her tablet, her laughter still lingering in the air from a few minutes earlier. Myra tried to join in, to stay in the rhythm, but her eyes flicked toward her laptop. The screen still glowed, Luna's smile frozen in a browser tab she hadn't meant to leave open.

Jordan didn't miss it. Her tone sharpened instantly. "What's that?"

Myra moved to close the tab, but the hesitation cost her. Jordan stepped closer, eyes catching the name before the screen went dark.

"Luna," Jordan said, her voice flat. "Who is she?"

Myra hesitated. "She's… an old friend."

Jordan scoffed, crossing her arms. "An old friend you've been looking up enough for it to show in our shared browser history?"

Myra sighed, her jaw tightening. "It's not what you think."

"Then explain it." Jordan didn't raise her voice, but the cold edge in it stung sharper than yelling.

Myra stood, the air suddenly too thick in the room. She walked to the window, arms crossed over her chest like armor. "Luna was important to me. She still is, in a way. But it's not romantic. It's... unfinished."

Jordan's brow furrowed. "You ghosted her."

Myra turned, eyes flashing. "I didn't know what else to do back then. I was with Nicole, drowning. Luna was the one thing that felt safe, and that made her terrifying."

Jordan nodded slowly, but her jaw clenched. "So you ran. And now what? You're circling back?"

"No," Myra said quickly. "I'm not trying to go back. I just... needed to see her face again. To remember who I was before everything got messy."

Jordan's eyes narrowed. "You say you want something real with me, but you've got one foot in the past and the other in avoidance. How's that supposed to work?"

Myra flinched. "You think I don't know that? I'm trying, Jordan."

She didn't move from the window, the city blurring at the edges of her vision. "You want to talk about honesty? Fine. Let's talk about Jamaica."

Jordan's jaw tensed. "What about it?"

Myra turned to face her. "You were off. Distant. You drank more. You disappeared on walks. You kept whispering with Rhailyn like I wasn't even there."

Jordan's eyes narrowed, but Myra pressed on.

"I wanted to ask what we were doing so many times. But I swallowed it. I told myself not to ruin the moment. I ignored what I felt because I didn't want to hear you say it wasn't real. But you knew. You felt it too."

Jordan shifted her weight. "I didn't say anything because I didn't know what you wanted."

"No," Myra said, stepping forward. "You didn't say anything because it was easier to pretend. You asked me to be emotionally available while you stayed behind your wine glass and your sarcasm."

Jordan flinched, just barely.

Myra shook her head. "You want vulnerability? Then let's be real. That trip was when I knew you weren't all the way in. You liked having me next to you, but I was never sure you actually saw me."

Jordan's silence was telling.

"And Rhailyn?" Myra added, voice tight. "I've been wondering since that night what was so secret you had to wait until I walked away to say it?"

Jordan looked away. "That wasn't about you."

"It felt like it was," Myra shot back. "It felt like I was watching you keep a piece of yourself tucked away. And I've done that too. I know what it looks like."

They stared at each other in the stillness, stripped of performance, stripped of pretense. Two people holding too much and finally dropping the weight.

Jordan's voice broke the silence, lower this time but laced with something raw. "It feels like I'm competing with ghosts I didn't even know existed."

Myra opened her mouth, but the words didn't come. The tangled truth felt too complicated to unravel in a single breath.

Jordan stepped back, shaking her head. "Do you even want this?" she asked, her voice softer now but heavy with emotion. "Because I've been all in from the start. But if you're not—if you're still holding on to her, or Nicole, or whoever else—just say it."

"I do want this," Myra said quickly, her voice cracking under the weight of her guilt. "Jordan, I swear, I want us. I just… I didn't realize how much of the past I was still carrying."

Jordan studied her, eyes searching for something Myra wasn't sure she could give. After a long pause, she let out a deep breath. "Okay," she said, tone steady but edged with resignation. "But I need you to figure out what you're carrying and why. Because I can't keep being the person who fixes you while you chase shadows."

Myra nodded, the guilt and tension suffocating. "I'll figure it out. I promise."

Jordan's lips curved into a small, sad smile as she picked up her tablet. "Good. Because I can't compete with someone who isn't even here, Myra."

Her words echoed in the now-silent room as she walked toward the door. Jordan paused, her hand lingering on the knob. Her back was still turned, but Myra saw her shoulders rise and fall with a shaky breath.

"I'm not the kind of person who begs to be chosen, Myra," she said, barely above a whisper. "So please don't make me feel like I have to."

"We've got a client meeting in thirty," Jordan added over her shoulder. "Get ready."

The door clicked shut behind her.

Myra stayed rooted to the spot, the sound ringing in her ears like an aftershock. She turned back to the window, her reflection blending with the cityscape outside. For a moment, she just stared at herself—at everything she wasn't saying, everything she'd been trying to outrun.

She had been so afraid of being hurt again that she hadn't realized how much she'd already hurt someone still standing in front of her. And maybe that was the problem: she was always looking back, trying to make sense of the wreckage, hoping it would explain why she kept feeling unwhole.

But the truth was simpler.

She wasn't here.

Not fully.

She had shown up with walls still half-built and expected Jordan to meet her with an open door. But Jordan wasn't perfect either. She had kept pieces of herself tucked away, dressed her distance up in charm and wit, and never really let Myra all the way in. They had both danced around the truth, both reached for closeness without ever letting themselves be seen entirely.

And now, standing in the quiet, Myra knew something had to give.

She had to stop running. Not for Jordan. Not for Luna. Not for anyone else. But for herself.

Because healing wasn't in the looking back. It was in the standing still, in the choosing.

And maybe that's what this was: a beginning that didn't look like one. A seed planted in the middle of a mess. Not the end, but a reckoning.

She exhaled and whispered, mostly to herself, "I'm still figuring it out."

Chapter 13
Healing Changed Me First

The condo was quiet. Not peaceful, just still. Like a breath held too long. Like something waiting to break.

Myra sat on the edge of the couch, arms draped over her knees, eyes locked on the untouched glass of wine on the coffee table. It was there for comfort, for normalcy. But now it just looked like a ritual she didn't have the energy to complete. The red liquid shimmered in the fading light, a mirror for everything she was holding back.

Jordan wasn't home yet. Myra had noticed the shifts not just in the space between them, but in the way silence had started answering questions they no longer asked.

The last few weeks had carved something open in her. After the confrontation, the raw, jagged honesty that left both of them exposed, Myra couldn't go back to pretending. So she didn't.

She ran in the mornings now, the city's rhythm syncing with her breath. She signed up for therapy—not the kind you quit after two sessions, but the kind where you sit through the discomfort and name your shame out loud. She journaled nightly, her handwriting uneven as she dug up memories she had buried too deep.

Work became her anchor. She led meetings with confidence, closed deals with ease, filled every hour with movement, motion, momentum. It was easier to stay busy than to sit with the ache in her chest that hadn't quite gone away.

Jordan noticed. Of course she did.

"You've been glowing lately," she said one morning, handing.

Myra a protein shake with a faint smile. "Focused. Sharp."

Myra nodded, grateful but unsure how to explain the ache behind her glow. "Just trying to keep moving forward."

Jordan didn't press. She rarely did anymore.

They still spent time together. Dinner. A show. A weekend trip they barely planned. But it all felt slightly out of sync, like a song they both remembered but couldn't find the right key for.

One night, Jordan lingered in the doorway as Myra packed up her laptop.

"Dinner?" she asked, casual but too careful.

Myra didn't look up. "I've got therapy. And a call after that." Jordan hesitated, then nodded. "Of course. Another night." But there wasn't another night. Not really. Just more of the same:

Myra healing on her own, Jordan watching from the outside.

It all came to a head in the kitchen, two weeks later.

Jordan leaned against the counter, arms folded across her chest. "You're doing great," she said, her voice steady but tired. "Really. I'm proud of you."

Myra glanced up from her phone. "Thanks."

"But where do I fit into all this?" Jordan's words were soft, almost too gentle, like she was afraid to shatter something that was already cracking.

Myra blinked. "What do you mean?"

Jordan took a breath. "I mean, I watch you wake up early, journal, go to therapy, run five miles before I even have coffee. You're growing. You're becoming this version of yourself that's strong and clear and grounded. And I'm standing here trying to figure out if there's still room for me in the picture."

Myra's throat tightened. "Of course there is. I'm doing this for me, but also for us."

Jordan nodded slowly. "It doesn't feel like us anymore. It feels like I'm cheering from the sidelines while you rebuild a life I'm no longer part of."

Myra stepped forward, unsure how to close the space between them. "I don't want you to feel that way."

Jordan offered a sad smile. "I know. But I do."

The silence returned—not angry, just aching.

Myra reached for Jordan's hand, but Jordan gently stepped back. Not out of spite, but self-preservation.

"I love that you're finding yourself," Jordan said, her voice barely above a whisper. "But I don't know if you're trying to find us."

That night, Myra sat alone in their living room. The wine glass was still untouched. Her journal sat open on the armrest, but the words wouldn't come.

For all the work she was doing—every mile, every therapy session, every late-night meditation—she hadn't figured out how to hold space for someone else.

She wanted to believe growth would lead to clarity, that healing would bring them closer.

But maybe healing meant letting go of what couldn't survive the process.

She closed her eyes. Jordan was right.

She was changing.

And she had no idea if Jordan still fit into the woman she was becoming.

Chapter 14
The Silence Left Behind

The shift was subtle at first, then undeniable. At work, Jordan stopped lingering in Myra's doorway.

She no longer brought her coffee the way she used to—no extra syrup, no hand on her shoulder during meetings. Their once-effortless rhythm became robotic. Straightforward. Efficient. Every exchange was businesslike: crisp, transactional, clipped.

Myra felt it in the way Jordan now called her Myra instead of Mai. She felt it in the dry tone of, "Your client is in Conference Myra," instead of, "Hey babe, your two o'clock's here." Whatever warmth they had built had been shelved.

Myra told herself it was fine—professional even. Cleaner. But every day that passed, the distance dug deeper into her ribs.

At home, they still tried. Dinner at the table. Conversations about the news. Shared groceries. But it felt like playing house with a roommate you used to love and didn't know how to love anymore. Jordan would ask how therapy was going, and Myra would give short answers. Myra would ask how Jordan slept, and Jordan would say fine—always fine.

They weren't fighting. But they weren't connecting either.

And the silence between them was no longer neutral, it was a wall. One night after work, they sat in the condo's living room, takeout spread between them. The TV played something neither was watching. Myra picked at her food, unsure whether to pretend everything was fine or finally say something.

Jordan beat her to it.

"Can I ask you something?"

Myra looked up, surprised. "Of course."

Jordan didn't sugarcoat. "Do you even see me anymore?"

The question punched the breath from Myra's lungs. "What?"

Jordan set down her chopsticks, her gaze steady. "At work, you treat me like just another assistant. At home, you're always somewhere else—your laptop, your journal, your runs. I know you're healing. I support that. But where do I fit now? Am I just someone who fills the space between your therapy appointments and your next breakthrough?"

Myra blinked, caught off guard by how direct it was. "That's not fair."

Jordan's tone didn't waver. "It's honest."

Myra stood, pacing. "I'm doing my best. You said you wanted me to work on myself, so I am."

"I said I wanted you to show up." Jordan's voice cracked slightly. "Not disappear behind your routines."

Myra turned toward her, arms crossed. "You knew I was broken when you met me."

Jordan's laugh was bitter and low. "Don't weaponize your healing like that. I didn't sign up to fix you, Myra. I just wanted to be chosen."

Silence filled the room like water in a sinking ship.

Myra's eyes stung. "So that's it? You're just walking away?"

Jordan shook her head slowly. "I already did. You just never noticed."

The next morning, Jordan walked into Myra's office with the same calm efficiency she always had. A manila folder was tucked beneath her arm. She placed it gently on the desk.

Myra looked up, heart already pounding. "What's that?"

Jordan's voice didn't waver. "My resignation."

Myra stood so fast her chair nearly tipped. "Wait. Jordan, no"

"I've been holding on, hoping we'd find our way back. But I realized I'm the only one reaching."

Myra moved around the desk, panic rising. "We can fix this. I'll do better—"

"I know you will," Jordan said, softer now. "But not with me. Not right now." "Please," Myra whispered, her voice cracking. "I don't want to lose you."

Jordan's hand brushed against Myra's for the briefest second, then slipped away. *"Goodbye, Myra," she said,*

And then she turned. Walked out of the office. Out of the job. Out of the last thread holding them together.

That night, Myra sat in the condo alone, the silence no longer just heavy, it was hollow. An ache she couldn't stretch out, couldn't jog away from, couldn't write her way through. Jordan's absence was everywhere.

She walked to the bookshelf and picked up the framed photo from the mountains, the two of them smiling like they had the world. She remembered how light she felt that day. How full. And now…

She held the frame for a long time before turning it facedown.

For the first time in years, Myra didn't distract herself. She didn't run from the ache, spiritualize it, or numb it with hustle. She sat in it.

Felt every bit of the loss.

Faced every version of herself she'd been running from. Jordan had walked away.

And maybe she needed to.

Because if Myra didn't face this silence now—really face it— she never would.

CHAPTER 15
THROUGH HER EYES

Luna stepped into the house, heels clicking softly against the pristine hardwood floors. The kind of silence that met her wasn't just luxurious—it was surgical. The air inside was cool, crisp, too well-curated to feel like a home.

But that wasn't what made her breath catch.

It was the faint echo of a presence she hadn't felt in five years:

Myra.

Luna smoothed her blazer as she followed Erica, through the entryway. The girl was bubbly, efficient, reciting square footage and ceiling heights like gospel. But Luna barely heard her. Her eyes scanned the space, searching, already bracing.

And there she was.

Myra stood near the base of the staircase, posture too poised, too polished. Like nothing had ever unraveled between them. Like she hadn't disappeared with no warning, no explanation— just a hollowed-out space where something sacred used to be.

She looked good. Of course she did. Sleek hair, tailored clothes, that quiet authority she always wore like perfume.

But Luna wasn't here for nostalgia.

She was here to see if her heart still flinched. Spoiler: it did.

Myra finally turned, mid-conversation with a contractor, and their eyes met. The effect was instant, like being jolted awake mid-dream.

"Luna," Myra said. Calm. Too calm.

Her voice landed soft but charged. Luna felt it everywhere—chest, spine, throat.

"Myra," she answered evenly, though her palms had gone clammy. "It's been a while."

Erica looked between them, sensing something but smiling anyway. "This is our Broker, Myra Edwards. She'll walk you through the space personally."

Myra didn't flinch. "Let's start in the kitchen."

Luna followed, but her mind was already spiraling. She'd imagined this moment too many times to count, and in none of them had Myra looked this composed—detached, even.

The kitchen was gorgeous, all clean lines and imported surfaces. Luna barely registered the details. She was too focused on Myra's hands as they grazed the countertop, and noticing the way she avoided looking directly at her for too long. Still playing it safe.

"So," Luna said, voice light but pointed, " is this your usual way of catching up with old friends? High-end listings and surface-level pleasantries?"

Myra's fingers paused mid-motion. Her eyes flicked up, unreadable. "Didn't know you'd be the client until this morning."

"And if you had?" Luna pressed, arms folded. "Would you have canceled the showing or just sent someone else to deal with it?"

"I don't know," Myra said after a beat. "But I'm here now."

Luna laughed, but it held no humor. "Classic. Always arriving late to what matters."

Erica reentered just then, clipboard in hand and energy bright like a wrong frequency. "Let me show you the walk-in pantry— "

"Give us a minute," Myra said smoothly, without looking at her.

Erica blinked. "Sure. I'll, um... be in the den."

Luna waited until the assistant's heels faded down the hallway before stepping in closer.

"You don't get to act like this is normal," she said. "Like we're just two professionals in a house."

Myra's jaw tightened. "I'm not acting."

"No?" Luna tilted her head. "You think I don't see it? The way you won't meet my eyes for more than three seconds? You're walking through this tour like I'm just some buyer, and not the person you ghosted mid-sentence five years ago."

Myra's posture stayed firm, but something in her gaze flickered. "You think I didn't pay for that silence every day since?"

"Not with me, you didn't." The words came out sharper than intended, but Luna didn't pull them back.

The silence that followed crackled. Finally, Myra took a breath.

"You look well."

"Don't do that," Luna said. "Don't throw compliments over the mess. Say what you actually want to say."

Myra hesitated. "What do you want me to say, Luna?"

"I want the truth. I want to know why I wasn't worth a goodbye. I want to know what version of yourself you thought you had to become to erase me."

Myra opened her mouth, then closed it. She looked out the window instead, the city skyline shining behind her like a perfect distraction.

From the hallway, Erica's voice echoed faintly. "Whenever you're ready to see the upstairs, I can, uh, jump back in."

Neither of them responded.

Luna let out a breath, gathering herself. Her expression softened, just a little. "Alright. Show me the rest of the house."

Myra nodded, and they walked.

They toured bedrooms and bathrooms, closets and corridors. But none of it landed. The only architecture that mattered was the one between them—walls they'd built, bricks made from the things they never said.

Still, every so often, their hands would brush. A glance would linger too long. Luna would feel it—the unfinished thing pulsing beneath their professionalism. By the time they reached the patio, the sun had dropped lower, painting the sky in bruised color.

Luna looked out over the skyline and asked, "Do you ever stop working?"

Myra blinked, caught off guard. "Excuse me?"

"You heard me. You talk like a brochure, Myra. Everything's polished. Perfect. Do you ever stop selling and actually live in anything you build?"

Myra's lips parted, like she might deflect, but something softened instead.

"Work is what keeps me upright."

"And what keeps you honest?" Luna asked.

Myra didn't answer. But in her silence, Luna found something close to the truth.

Maybe this wasn't closure. Maybe it wasn't a reunion. But it was a beginning of something more real than before. Because this time, Luna wasn't the one pretending.

They walked the rest of the house without needing to fill every space with words. Conversation came easier now—lighter, small jokes, shared glances, the kind of ease that only came from history. For a moment, it felt like they'd slipped into something familiar. But beneath it all, the tension still hummed—not anger anymore, something more fragile. The weight of everything left unspoken.

As they stood near the front door, Luna turned slightly, ready to go. But Myra stopped her, voice soft.

"Would you come by the office with me?" she asked. "I know we're not done here, and I want to talk without the noise."

Luna studied her for a beat—this version of Myra who looked composed but not quite settled. And she nodded.

"Lead the way."

Luna didn't rush to follow Myra's car when the showing ended.

She took her time pulling away from the property, needing a few extra moments to breathe, to ground herself. The house had been beautiful, sure, but that wasn't what had rattled her. It was everything unspoken that clung to the air long after Myra had walked her through vaulted ceilings and marble counters, like they hadn't once shared something deeper than square footage.

By the time she arrived at Myra's office, her pulse had mostly settled. Mostly.

She parked, sat for a moment behind the wheel, then finally made her way inside.

Myra was already there, wine already poured. That alone told Luna everything: this wasn't going to be light. This wasn't going to be one of Myra's polished updates with a tight smile and casual charm. This was something else.

Too much had gone unsaid for too long.

Myra's office was sleek—of course it was. Minimalist décor, perfectly stacked books, a framed abstract painting that probably cost more than Luna's first car. Everything about the space screamed curation, not comfort. Just like Myra.

Luna turned in her seat, watching the woman across from her.

Myra was talking, trying to explain. The words were raw, vulnerable even, but Luna couldn't help but notice the practiced rhythm in Myra's voice, the kind people used when they'd rehearsed the truth enough times to believe it themselves.

She heard her say things like, "I didn't want to leave anything unsaid this time," and "I know I hurt you."

And part of Luna wanted to believe it was enough, that Myra showing her cards was the closure she'd waited on for years. But it wasn't.

Because something in Myra's apology still felt like it was being told through glass—pretty, distant, refracted just enough to make it safe.

Luna sipped her wine, the coolness of the glass grounding her. "You thought you were protecting me," she murmured, her voice steadier than she felt. "But you never gave me a choice in that. You decided for both of us."

Myra flinched, barely, but it was enough.

"I know," she whispered. "And I hate myself for that."

For the first time, Luna saw it—the fracture in Myra's perfectly polished exterior. She looked tired. Not in the way work tired you, but in the way silence did, in the way carrying secrets too long eventually bent your spine.

Luna almost softened. But then the door opened. And just like that, the air in the room changed.

Luna didn't have to guess who the woman was. She knew the second Myra tensed, her spine straightening like a soldier hearing an old command.

Jordan.

She walked in like she owned the space, like she knew exactly what she was interrupting and didn't care. "I just thought I'd drop by," Jordan said with a smirk, eyes dancing between them. "Didn't know I'd be interrupting something."

You did, Luna thought. That's exactly why you're here. "You are," Myra said flatly, standing up.

Jordan's smirk widened. "I see that."

Then she turned to Luna. "You must be the infamous Luna."

Luna didn't flinch. "And you must be the reason Myra's been walking around like she forgot who she was."

Jordan blinked, taken aback for the briefest moment.

Myra stepped between them, voice sharp. "Jordan, not now."

Jordan held up her hands. "Relax. I just needed a signature."

Myra snatched the folder from her hands, signed it without sitting down, and handed it back. "There. Now leave."

Jordan took it, but lingered. Of course she did.

"You know," she said, turning back to Luna, "Myra and I go way back."

Luna smiled tightly. "So does trauma. Doesn't mean you hold on to it."

Jordan's expression flickered, but she didn't reply. She looked at Myra one last time before finally turning and walking out. The door clicked shut.

Myra exhaled, her fingers brushing through her hair. "I'm sorry about that."

Luna stared at her. "She's still got a hold on you." "No," Myra said, too fast. "Not in the way you think."

"Then why does she walk in here like she still owns something?"

Myra paused. And that pause told Luna everything.

"It's complicated," Myra said quietly.

Luna let out a hollow laugh. "Of course it is."

Myra looked down at her glass. "I don't want her."

Luna leaned forward, her voice low and sharp. "Are you sure?"

Myra's lips parted, but no words came out. For once, she had nothing polished, nothing prepared. Just silence.

And this time, it wasn't tender. It was telling.

Luna sat back, her pulse still steady but her heart racing. She wasn't seventeen anymore. She wasn't soft enough to be soothed by apology and chemistry. She needed truth.

And Myra, for all her grace and evolution, still wasn't quite ready to bleed for it.

But Luna was watching now—not with rose-colored eyes, but with clarity. And she wouldn't be the one waiting in the shadows this time.

Myra let out a slow breath, her fingers trailing over the rim of her glass. "You didn't have to stay."

Luna's gaze flicked toward her, the edge in her expression softening just a touch. "Didn't say I came back to fix anything."

Myra nodded, a faint smile ghosting her lips. "Still… I'm glad you did."

The tension lingered thick, unsaid but no longer sharp enough to draw blood. Just a quiet ache hanging in the air between them.

Luna leaned back slightly, arms crossed, but her posture had eased. "You still talk in riddles," she murmured, not unkindly.

"And you still pretend you're not curious," Myra shot back, her tone a little lighter now.

A breath passed. Then another. It wasn't laughter, but it was something close. Almost familiar.

Myra reached for her phone, avoiding Luna's eyes. "You eat yet?"

"Yes I did before I came."

Myra tapped her screen, then looked up, eyes meeting Luna's for the briefest moment. "You want to grab brunch tomorrow?"

Luna raised a brow, surprised. "That your way of apologizing?"

Myra shrugged. "It's my way of saying I don't want this to end here. That's all I've got tonight."

Luna didn't answer right away. She rose slowly, already halfway to the door when she finally said, 'I'll think about it.'

Myra watched her go, her heart thudding behind her ribs.

CHAPTER 16
THE WEIGHT OF BEING SEEN

Beep-beep-beep. Beep-beep-beep.

Myra's hand reached blindly across the nightstand, silencing the alarm with a lazy slap. The room was still dim, the sun only beginning to bleed through her sheer curtains in soft, golden streaks. She stayed there for a moment, motionless, quiet, letting the silence wrap around her like a blanket she wasn't ready to shake off.

Last night played behind her eyes like a slow reel: the wine. The tension. Luna. The way her name still sat heavy and sweet in the center of Myra's chest.

She was here. Back. Maybe not entirely, not securely, but she was here.

And Myra hadn't dreamed it. A tentative smile crept across her face. For once, waking up didn't feel like bracing for impact. Instead, it felt like the moment right before spring: still fragile, still cold, but full of promise.

She swung her legs over the edge of the bed and moved toward the bathroom. The mirror met her with something unfamiliar— not just the typical morning puffiness or pillow-creased cheek. No, there was something else in her reflection: a softness around the eyes, a weight that had lifted, if only slightly.

Hope, she realized. And fear, too, tangled right beside it. She turned on the shower, stepping into the steam like it could rinse off everything she didn't yet have the words for—the what-ifs, the should-haves, the still-coulds. The water ran hot, but her thoughts ran hotter.

What happens now?

By the time she walked into the office, Myra had tucked the night's emotions neatly behind her ribcage. Back to business. Back to composed. She wore a blazer today—not just for style, but for armor.

Erica caught her first.

"Did everything turn out well?" she asked, her voice laced with curiosity just barely masked by professionalism.

Myra paused mid-step, caught off guard. "What do you mean?"

she asked, too evenly.

Erica gave her a slow once-over, smirking. "You're energy feels different this morning. So I'm gonna take that as a yes."

Heat bloomed at the back of Myra's neck, betraying the practiced calm in her tone. She offered a polite, too-quick smile. "Good morning to you, too," she quipped, stepping into her office and closing the door behind her with a soft thud.

A few hours passed, the morning slipping by in a steady rhythm of emails, calls, and calendar blocks. Myra buried herself in the busyness, grateful for the structure—grateful, even, for the distractions. But under the clicking keyboard and muted conference calls, the echoes of last night lingered: the conversation, the stare, the silence that wasn't quite empty.

She hadn't let herself sit with it for too long. That wasn't how she operated. Feelings stayed folded. Work came first.

Still, every so often, her eyes drifted to the untouched second glass of wine on the credenza across the room. She hadn't poured it for herself.

She was halfway through drafting an offer when the knock came—soft but distinct, three taps like a signature she hadn't heard in years.

Before she could respond, the sound of quick footsteps neared. Erica's heels clicked against the hallway tile as she rushed toward the door, eyes wide.

"Sorry!" she whispered just before the handle turned. "I forgot I was supposed to give you a heads-up." But it was too late.

Erica opened the door, and behind her stood Luna.

The moment their eyes met, the air in the room deepened. Myra felt her pulse quicken as Luna's gaze locked onto hers with an intensity that made her knees weak. For a moment, the room was silent, save for the faint hum of the office beyond.

Myra stood slowly, smoothing her blouse in a futile attempt to mask the sudden tension coiling in her chest.

"Hey," she said softly, the single word carrying far more weight than it should have. Luna didn't smile, but she didn't turn away either.

"Hey," she replied, stepping inside.

The air between them thrummed—electric, charged with emotion.

"Rightttt," Erica said quickly, as if suddenly remembering she was still standing there. She adjusted the tablet in her arms, her tone too bright. "I saw you hadn't checked your messages this morning, so I went ahead and sorted through them. Just a few confirmations for showings tomorrow and… a message from a woman named Jordan.”

Myra froze.

Luna didn't move, but Myra saw it—the subtle stiffening of her shoulders, the way her jaw tensed ever so slightly.

“She said she'd like to meet with you later this week,” Erica continued, flipping through her notes. “Said 'when everything turns out like she expected.' She's available Thursday.”

Silence cracked through the room.

Jordan's name still had the power to pull, but the weight of it was gone. Whatever they'd been—it was over now. Entirely.

Erica's voice faltered. “I… I can reschedule, if needed…”

Myra's mouth opened, but no sound came out. Luna glanced away, eyes narrowing just enough to make the discomfort tangible.

“No,” Myra said finally, her voice quieter than she intended. “It's fine.”

Erica lingered, clearly sensing she had stepped into something thick and personal.

Luna's lips curved into a tight smile. “I just wanted to say yes to brunch. Are you ready? I'm starving,” she said pointedly, her voice cutting through the tension like a knife.

Myra's lips twitched at the abruptness, her chest loosening just enough to let a breath escape. “Was that what you came back here for? I figured we'd just meet there… so now I'm just gonna assume this is a date?” she teased, tilting her head, keeping her tone playful even if her heart had already kicked into overdrive.

Erica, still awkwardly hovering near the door, blinked at the shift in energy. Her gaze ping-ponged between them before it clicked.

"Oh. Right. I'll just…" She motioned vaguely toward the hallway, a knowing smile creeping onto her face. "Yeah. I'll be at my desk."

Luna smirked as the door clicked softly shut behind her.

Silence returned, but this time, it felt warmer—charged, but not dangerous. Just… new.

Myra's blush deepened, and she turned away to grab her jacket, hoping to hide the flutter in her chest. "You're impossible," she muttered, brushing past Luna and heading for the door, her tone clipped but betraying a smile.

From the hallway, Luna's voice followed, teasing, warm, and unbothered. "Now you wanna act shy?"

Myra stopped in her tracks and turned, her eyes narrowing with a mix of exasperation and amusement. "I'm not shy. I just don't like my assistant being all up in my business. I'm a private person."

Luna stepped closer, closing the space between them, her voice dipping lower. "I'm not one of your employees, Myra. I'm your friend."

A pause.

Then, quieter: "And I don't even want to be just that."

Myra froze, breath caught in her throat. Her heart pounded so loudly she was sure Luna could hear it. "What do you mean?" she asked, her voice barely above a whisper.

Luna's eyes softened as she reached out, her fingers lightly brushing Myra's arm before gently turning her to face her. "I thought a lot about what we talked about last night," she said, voice steady but intimate. "And I realized… we're standing in a moment right now. One where we can actually choose to work through this. Not skip past it. Not bury it. But actually move through it together."

Myra's breath caught. The sincerity in Luna's tone hit her like a wave—so grounding, so real it almost hurt. Her hands trembled at her sides.

But her mind betrayed her.

Cracks spidered through her composure, the weight of her insecurities pressing hard against her chest. She's here. She's serious. Why does that scare me more than it comforts me? The questions clawed at her ribs, threatening to unravel her from the inside.

But Luna's presence didn't flinch. She stood steady. Solid. Eyes locked on Myra with a quiet kind of knowing that made it impossible to run.

"Luna, I…" Myra's voice broke on the edge of the words. She turned her face slightly, trying to hide the fracture in her expression. The storm inside her was loud—too loud to name.

Luna tilted her head, catching Myra's eyes again. "You don't have to explain anything right now," she said gently. "You just have to let me in."

Something in Myra stilled. The storm didn't vanish, but it softened—just enough to let her breathe.

Her lips parted, but still, the words wouldn't come. So she nodded. Small. Barely there. But real. And it was enough.

Luna's mouth curved into a soft smile as she reached out, her fingers grazing Myra's—slow, certain, warm. The contact sent a quiet jolt up Myra's spine. Not lust. Not fear. Something else. Something that whispered: You're safe.

"Come on," Luna said, her voice low and light. "Let's go to brunch before I pass out."

Myra exhaled, something like laughter—like release—bubbling up in her chest.

The café hummed with a soft weekend rhythm: espresso machines whirring, silverware clinking, low conversations drifting beneath a mellow Lunaz playlist. Sunlight filtered through gauzy curtains, casting golden stripes across the worn wood floor and the corner booth where Myra and Luna had settled.

Myra tucked herself into the window seat, back straight, shoulders pulled taut. She picked up the menu like it was a shield, flipping it open and pretending to study it with intense interest. The pages barely moved, her eyes never quite focusing on the words.

Luna didn't bother hiding her amusement. She lounged across from Myra, chin in hand, watching her over the top of her own untouched menu. Her gaze was steady, playful at first but sharpening with intent.

"Are you really going to read that entire menu just to dodge me?" Luna asked, her voice low and teasing, laced with challenge. She leaned in slightly, elbows resting on the table.

Myra didn't look up. "I'm deciding what to eat."

"You've been on the pancake page for five minutes," Luna pointed out, a smirk tugging at her lips. "You're not hungry. You're hiding."

Myra's fingers tightened around the menu. "I'm not hiding. I'm multitasking."

Luna arched a brow. 'Right. Multitasking. Classic Myra. But listen—I'm really here right now, and I need you to stop pretending this is just brunch.

Myra finally looked up, caught off guard by the shift in Luna's tone. "What are you about to say?" she asked slowly, brow knitting.

Luna didn't blink. 'I need you to hear me. So for once, don't talk. Don't deflect. Just listen until I'm done.'

Myra blinked, surprised by the directness. She set the menu down carefully, hands folding in her lap. "Okay…"

Luna exhaled, the playful edge melting into something rawer. "Good. Because I didn't come here just to eat. I came here to lay it all out."

Myra crossed her arms, leaning back against the cushioned booth. Her brow lifted with mock defiance, but the edge in her expression softened just a bit. "You're not the same Luna from five years ago," she said, voice low. "Well… maybe you are. Just sharper. Louder in your truth."

Luna leaned in, her tone steady but vulnerable. "I want to be with you, Myra. I'm not gonna lie about that. But I want to start by taking things slow."

Her words hung heavy in the air, their eyes locking, frustration and unspoken emotions swirling between them.

The tension was thick, almost tangible, when the waiter approached the table, menus in hand. He paused, eyes flicking between the two of them like he'd just walked in on a movie mid- climax.

"Uh…" he said slowly, trying to sound casual. "Should I… clock in as your couples therapist or just get your drink orders?"

Luna cracked a grin despite herself, and Myra let out the smallest laugh, the tension loosening just a little at the edges.

Myra looked over at Luna, her eyes softer now. "Luna, I want to try this. I really do."

Luna scooted a little closer in the booth, her voice dipping playfully. "We can start slow," she said, lips curling into a grin. "I'll just have to learn to keep my hands to myself."

Myra arched an eyebrow, teasing. "I'll work on it too."

"Good. Now," Luna said, casting a glance toward the waiter who still lingered like he was waiting for a commercial break, "can we order so he doesn't have to keep listening to our craziness?"

The waiter, caught between professionalism and eavesdropping, blinked back to life and pulled out his notepad. "Y'all ready for drinks, or should I grab an application for a couples therapist?"

Myra stifled a laugh as Luna waved a dismissive hand. "We'll order. Promise."

The waiter took their drink orders and asked about entrées, but before either of them could respond, Myra leaned in slightly, her voice low and full of mischief. "Kiss me, so I know it's real."

Luna blinked, caught off guard by the shift in tone, her cheeks flushing. "You kiss me, so I know you really do want this."

The waiter, clearly regretting not walking away faster, shook his head. "You two are gonna starve at this rate."

Luna burst out laughing, rich and unbothered. "Don't worry. I'll order while she keeps staring at me for not giving her a kiss."

Myra groaned, burying her face in her hands as Luna confidently rattled off both of their orders. When the waiter finally disappeared, Myra peeked through her fingers, eyes narrowed.

"You're impossible."

"And yet," Luna said, leaning back with a smug smirk, "here we are."

Myra rolled her eyes but couldn't hide the smile tugging at her lips. Whatever they were stepping into, it was messy, uncertain… but maybe, just maybe, worth it.

Their food arrived with a quiet clatter of plates and silverware. Myra barely waited for the waiter to step back before grabbing the syrup and dousing her pancakes without an ounce of remorse. The golden cascade soaked into the stack and spilled over the sides like a sugary waterfall.

Luna stared, wide-eyed. "Damn, Myra. What did those pancakes ever do to you?"

Myra smirked. "They looked dry."

Before she could take a bite, the waiter reappeared, catching sight of the scene. He raised a brow with mock concern. "You want pancakes with that syrup?"

Luna broke into laughter, her head falling back as she clutched her stomach. Myra rolled her eyes and jabbed her fork into the syrup-soaked stack. "You two should start a comedy tour."

Luna wiped a tear from her eye, still giggling. "You're the one turning breakfast into a pool party."

Myra shot her a side-eye but couldn't suppress the grin tugging at her lips.

As the laughter faded, Luna's expression shifted. She cut into her omelet slowly, thoughtfully. "So… this," she said, glancing up. "You really want to give it a real shot?"

Myra paused mid-chew, then set her fork down. Her tone was quieter now, more honest.

"I do. I really do. But I don't want to rush into something just to lose it all over again."

Luna nodded, letting the weight of that truth land. "Fair. But for the record," she said, her gaze steady, "I'm not going anywhere." She leaned in slightly. "And you better not go anywhere this time, Myra."

That landed deeper than Myra expected. Her chest tightened, but not in fear, in recognition. In hope. "Okay," she said softly, almost like a vow.

Luna reached across the table, fingers brushing against Myra's in a quiet, grounding touch. "Fast, slow, doesn't matter to me," she said. "We've got time. What matters is we're both in it."

Myra nodded, feeling the tension inside her finally loosen its grip.

They ate in easy silence after that, no more pressure, no more pretending. Just two women relearning how to sit across from each other without the weight of five years between them.

As Myra wiped her mouth and leaned back, Luna glanced over at her, thoughtful.

"I didn't think I'd ever be sitting here again. Not like this," Luna admitted. "But now that I am... I want to see where it goes. As long as we keep it slow."

Myra gave a quiet, knowing smile. "I can respect that," she replied, her voice steady but sincere. "And because of that… I'll let you set the pace."

Luna gave a small, appreciative smile. "Let's start with dating first."

"And save the mind-blowing sex with the longest-lasting orgasm I'll ever have for later," Luna added casually, eyes sparkling with mischief.

Myra's eyebrow shot up, but her lips twitched into a teasing grin. "You'll ever have?" she repeated, her voice dipping into a flirtatious drawl.

The confidence slipped just a little as Myra's cheeks warmed, her expression giving her away. She turned her face slightly, trying to hide the heat creeping up her neck.

"Are you always this shy?" Luna countered, chuckling. Her tone held no judgment, just warmth, like she was genuinely enjoying watching Myra squirm a little.

Before Myra could answer, the waiter returned with the check and two neatly stacked to-go boxes. "Here you go, ladies," he said with a polite smile, setting them on the table.

"Thanks," Myra said, reaching for the check and sliding one box across the table toward Luna. She hesitated for half a second, just long enough to catch Luna watching her. And not just watching, looking. The kind of look that made her knees feel unreliable. The kind of look that said, I've thought about kissing you all morning.

Myra blinked, swallowed, and stood a little too quickly. "Ready?" "Always," Luna said with a smirk.

They stepped out into the midday sun, the buzz of the café giving way to the quieter rhythm of the sidewalk. As they made their way toward the office, the space between them wasn't awkward, but it was loaded. Soft tension. Possibility.

Myra broke the silence first. "So…" she started, glancing sideways. "Are we defining this or…"

Luna didn't answer right away. She slowed her pace, the air between them suddenly charged with something heavier.

"I don't know," she said honestly. "If we define this, if I say I'm with you, then you're attached to me. In the eyes of everybody."

Myra frowned slightly. "Isn't that… kind of the point of a relationship? To be with someone openly?"

Luna sighed, running a hand through her curls as they walked slowly back toward the office. "Okay, let me try to explain that better," she said, her tone thoughtful. "If you and I start showing up in public as a couple, there's going to be a story ready before we even sit down. Headlines like 'Luna's Mystery Boo' or 'Luna Has a Girlfriend, Who Knew She Was Gay?' And then your office gets flooded with calls from people trying to figure out who you are. Your name, your job, your life… it won't be just yours anymore. You get it?"

Myra's brows furrowed, but her expression slowly softened as the weight of Luna's words settled. "Got it," she said quietly. "It'll go public. Especially because of the 'girlfriend' part."

Luna nodded, but her gaze lingered on Myra's face, searching. "But how is this just my decision?" she asked, a slight edge of frustration creeping in. "Do you not have any concerns about defining this? About being seen with me?"

Myra shook her head without hesitation. "No," she said firmly. "I've wanted to be with you for so long. I'll take whatever comes. If it means staying out of the spotlight, I'll do it. If it means hiding until you're ready, I'll do that too. Just so I can be with you."

That answer didn't settle Luna. Not completely.

"Which would you prefer, though?" she asked, her voice quieter now, more vulnerable.

Myra looked down, her fingers tightening slightly around her to- go box. She exhaled slowly. "I'd prefer not to have to fight the urge to touch you," she admitted, her voice barely above a whisper. "Because that's going to be hell. I've become… a very affectionate person, Luna."

Luna's chest rose and fell with a slow breath, the tension in her shoulders visible. A relationship with Myra, something she had dreamed about and mourned in silence, suddenly felt like both the most beautiful risk and the most fragile one. The weight of being seen, of being known, of being claimed in a world that didn't always play fair pressed heavy against her.

"You're right," she said finally, her voice low. "It's going to be a lot."

Myra hesitated then, her steps slowing. Something changed in her posture, nervousness edging its way in. She bit her lip, her eyes flicking sideways. "Just to start with honesty… there's something you should know."

Luna turned to face her more fully, eyebrows lifting. "What is it?"

Myra looked away, a nervous flutter in her chest. "Something you might not be thrilled to hear later if it comes from someone else."

Luna's gaze sharpened. "Myra... what is it?"

Myra crossed her arms, her eyes flicking downward with a hint of embarrassment. "The last few months..." she began, then sighed. "Without Jordan, I might've been... kind of a hoe."

Luna blinked, caught between confusion and amusement. "A hoe?" she echoed, leaning in like she hadn't heard right.

Myra nodded, wincing a little. "Yeah. I've been enjoying the single life, let's just say. It's been... an opportunity."

Luna's eyebrows arched. "How many women are we talking about here?"

Myra hesitated, her voice dropping to barely a whisper.

"Maybe... three?"

Luna went still. Her jaw tightened, the number settling somewhere sharp in her chest. Jealousy flared, wild and immediate. She clenched her jaw, struggling to swallow it down. "Three," she repeated slowly, like she was trying to make peace with the word.

Myra caught the shift, the tension radiating off Luna, and couldn't help the smile tugging at her lips. "Well, I guess you're going to have to be a little possessive then."

Luna smirked, though her eyes still burned with the heat of something primal. "I know," she muttered, her voice tinged with a low growl.

Myra's grin widened. "You've always been possessive. But I don't mind. Despite my... extracurriculars, I actually enjoy being claimed."

That softened Luna. Her posture relaxed slightly, though she was still clearly processing the honesty that had just been dropped in her lap.

"Even though we're not defining this yet," she said, her tone gentler now, "I appreciate the reassurance. And just so you know… it's reciprocated."

Myra looked at her then, really looked, and felt something loosen in her chest. She beamed at the woman in front of her, her heart fluttering at the sight of Luna: guarded, a little off-balance, but still fiercely protective.

She liked this version of her. She liked them. We're taking it slow, Myra reminded herself. And for once, that didn't scare her.

Slow was already proving to be anything but boring.

CHAPTER 17
WHERE WE START AGAIN

Myra didn't text Luna first, not because she didn't want to, but because this time, she wanted to do it right.

No pressure. No expectation. Just… something honest. So she sent a voice note.

"Okay, random question," Myra's voice came through Luna's phone, a little breathless, like she was mid-walk or pacing in her kitchen. "If you could only eat one cereal for the rest of your life, what would it be? And no, you can't say granola. That doesn't count."

It was the kind of message best friends sent each other. Light. Easy. Safe.

The reply came hours later, long after Luna had finished back-to-back clients and wiped off her makeup for the night. A sleepy voice note dropped into Myra's inbox, her laugh low and raspy from the day.

"First of all," Luna said, dragging the words like she was stretching them out in bed, "granola is elite. Don't do her like that. But… Cinnamon Toast Crunch. Final answer. Fight me."

It started like that.

The getting-to-know-you-again stage.

No grand declarations. No meetups with sparks flying. Just the steady rhythm of two people learning how to orbit each other without crashing this time.

They didn't hang out every day. Their lives didn't suddenly pause to make room for each other. But in the pockets of stillness between meetings and makeup sessions, Myra and Luna reached for each other.

A shared playlist called Us, But Slower. Random memes at 11:42 p.m.

Photos from years ago that made them both cringe and laugh.

Luna sent a video of a street performer singing Myra's favorite 2000s R&B throwback with the caption: Tell me this ain't you every time wine touches your lips.

Myra replied two seconds later:

Don't play. That is me. In my soul. Extra runs and all. Some nights, they didn't talk at all.

And those nights weren't awkward, they were safe.

A simple Made it home text.

A heart emoji sent during a particularly long day.

A soft Goodnight, Mai that lingered longer than it should have.

Instead of rushing into dinner dates or late-night drinks, Myra and Luna did something softer.

They did what best friends do.

They eased into a rhythm stitched together by small, ordinary moments. A slow rebuild that didn't need grand declarations, just presence.

Saturday mornings turned into coffee walks. They'd meet just after sunrise at the edge of the park, each holding their own overpriced drink: Myra's with extra syrup, Luna's always iced. They walked without destination, letting their shoes scrape through fallen leaves and sidewalk cracks while their conversations zigzagged between real estate deals, makeup launches, weird dreams, and why there were never enough trash cans in public spaces.

Sometimes they went to bookstores together. The cozy kind with uneven shelves and handwritten staff picks. They browsed in separate aisles, texting each other funny book titles from two rows away, only to reunite at the checkout line, arguing over who got to buy the last copy of a poetry collection they both wanted.

"I saw it first," Myra would say.

"But I picked it up first," Luna would counter.

They'd settle it like grownups: rock, paper, scissors. Myra never won. Not once.

Nights were quieter. Random FaceTime calls would appear on their screens around 9:47 p.m. No warnings. No expectations. Just Luna in her bonnet, curled up on the couch with a bowl of cereal, and Myra half-draped in a robe, scrolling Zillow listings.

"Why are you whispering?" Myra would ask.

"Because I'm pretending to be mysterious," Luna would grin.

Other nights, they didn't talk at all. They'd stay on the phone in silence, the glow of their screens the only thing holding them together. One of them would fall asleep mid-call, and the other wouldn't hang up, just listening to the soft rhythm of breathing until it was time to say goodnight.

This was how they re-learned each other, not as old lovers trying to rewind, but as two women standing in the present, slowly building something steady.

One night, Luna sent a text that landed softly but carried weight:

"Come over? No expectations. I just want to watch Forever and talk shit about how emotionally unwell everybody is."

Myra didn't hesitate.

She showed up with popcorn in one hand and a fuzzy blanket in the other, her face bare and her hair tied up like she hadn't even tried to impress. Because this wasn't about that. Not tonight.

Luna opened the door in sweatpants and an oversized hoodie, her locs pulled into a messy bun, and an easy smile on her face.

"You brought popcorn? Good." She smiled.

They curled up on the couch like old times. Two bowls. One remote. Endless commentary.

For the next two hours, they laughed, paused the show to dissect emotional breakdowns, overanalyzed each character's spiritual crisis, quoted the most dramatic one-liners before they happened, and took turns throwing popcorn whenever someone ghosted their healing journey.

At one point, Luna got so deep in her critique, she stood up and reenacted a whole scene from episode four, complete with a fake ugly cry and a monologue about emotional accountability. Myra laughed so hard her stomach hurt.

And somewhere between Keisha's spiraling and Justin acting emotionally unavailable for the fifth time, Myra looked over—at Luna's legs tucked underneath her, eyes wide and animated, hands gesturing mid-rant—and felt it.

Peace.

It was this. The friendship. The honesty.

The part where they could just be, without performing. Myra exhaled for what felt like the first time in years.

And Luna? She didn't have to say anything. She just nudged Myra's shoulder and muttered, "We still got it."

Later that night, after the popcorn bowl was nearly empty and the credits for Forever were rolling, the energy between them softened. The laughter faded into something quieter, comfortable, reflective.

Myra pulled the blanket up around her shoulders and glanced at Luna, who was lazily tracing the rim of her mug with her finger.

In one of their quieter moments, Myra finally asked, "What's your favorite version of yourself right now?"

Luna blinked, caught off guard. "Damn. You really asking Oprah questions now?"

Myra smirked, then nudged her gently. "I'm serious."

Luna paused, letting the silence stretch. Her eyes flicked toward the ceiling, then back to Myra.

"The version that wakes up every day and still shows up," she said finally. "Even when she doesn't want to. That one."

Myra nodded slowly, her voice low. "That's a good one." It wasn't glamorous. It wasn't dramatic. But it was real.

From that night on, things felt different, but in the quietest ways.

Myra started noticing how Luna took her coffee now: black with a splash of oat milk and honey. Luna learned that Myra couldn't function before 9 a.m. unless a playlist was already going— usually something soulful, always something nostalgic.

They teased. They bantered. They listened—really listened.

It wasn't about falling back in love.

It was about rediscovering each other, learning each other's rhythms again.

Discovering if they could build something new on purpose, with intention, without skipping steps this time.

And for once, neither of them was in a rush. They were just…in it.

Together.

Spring crept in with a full schedule and no apologies.

Luna's calendar was packed with makeup classes, wedding clients, and product launches. Meanwhile, Myra was drowning in showings, contract negotiations, and the early signs of her next big real estate flip. Texts slowed down. FaceTimes got shorter. Their playful voice notes turned into quiet likes and delayed replies.

It wasn't distance, just life.

So Myra didn't text first. She just showed up.

No warning, no "on my way" message. Just her, standing outside Luna's studio with a smoothie in one hand and a takeout bag in the other. She hadn't seen her in over a week.

Inside, the studio buzzed with energy. Luna moved like the center of gravity in the room, giving instructions, demonstrating brush strokes, tilting a client's chin just slightly with practiced ease. Her voice carried—calm but clear— threading confidence through the controlled chaos around her.

Myra waited by the entrance, content to watch. She wasn't there for anything. Just… to be there.

Eventually, Luna caught sight of her. A slow smile spread across her face, tired but genuine.

"Wow," she said as she made her way over, eyes dropping to the smoothie and bag. "You come bearing gifts?"

"I come in peace," Myra replied, holding them out like an offering. "Thought you might be too busy to eat."

Luna took the smoothie, eyeing her with something softer than surprise. "You thought right."

"I won't stay," Myra added quickly. "I just… hadn't seen your face in a while." That was all it took.

A look passed between them, unspoken but loud. I miss you, too.

"Wait in my office," Luna said, already turning back toward her assistants. "I've got like twenty more minutes."

Myra nodded and slipped into the back room. The walls were filled with mood boards, old Polaroids, and scribbled affirmations. Don't dim your light, one sticky note read in all caps. She sat in the worn chair by the desk, sipping from Luna's backup water bottle, flipping idly through a makeup manual left open on the armrest.

When Luna finally came in, she exhaled like she'd been holding her breath all day.

"Sorry," she said, kicking off her shoes. "It's been nonstop."

Myra stood, handing her the food. "You're good. I just wanted to see you in your element."

Luna raised an eyebrow. "Stalker vibes, but okay."

Myra laughed. "Inspirational stalker, maybe."

They both smiled, then fell into a comfortable quiet as Luna opened the bag, the smell of warm noodles filling the room. Myra leaned back in the chair again, tucking one leg under the other, watching Luna eat like it was the first real meal she'd had all day.

After a few moments, Myra spoke casually. "The construction crew's almost done with the house we toured."

Luna looked up mid-bite. "The one with the double front doors and the ugly chandelier?"

Myra laughed. "Exactly. I made them take the chandelier out the second I got the keys."

"Good," Luna said, nodding approvingly. "I hated that thing."

Myra reached for her water. "They're just finishing up the backsplash in the kitchen and replacing a few of the deck boards out back. After that, it's just the final inspection and walkthroughs."

Luna wiped her mouth with a napkin, then leaned over to grab her tablet from the desk.

"I actually went through the contract again last night, the one you sent me for the purchase."

Myra straightened, interest piqued. "Yeah?"

"I signed it," Luna said, setting the tablet down carefully. "But I had some questions. A few things didn't quite add up with the closing timeline and the title company."

Myra smiled, something warm settling in her chest. "Of course you do. I was hoping you'd catch that."

Luna raised an eyebrow. "You testing me?"

"Maybe a little," Myra teased. "But mostly, I just know you don't miss things. And I wanted you to really sit with it, make sure you felt good about everything."

Luna leaned back, crossing one leg over the other. "I do. Mostly. But I'm going to want to walk the house again before closing. Alone. Just to… feel it."

Myra nodded slowly. "Whenever you're ready."

The air between them shifted—not tense, but real. Tangible. Like the weight of this next step had quietly arrived, and neither of them needed to rush to carry it.

"Thanks for trusting me with this," Myra added softly.

Luna gave her a long look, the edges of her expression softening.

"Thanks for showing up today."

Neither said what they both felt, but it lingered in the quiet between them. This wasn't just a house. It was a beginning.

Myra gave a faint smile, her gaze lingering.

And maybe it was the way Luna's curls had fallen loose around her face, or how the office light hit just right, casting a honeyed glow across her cheekbones. Maybe it was the ease between them again, or the courage Myra finally felt sitting still in her chest.

She stood up slowly.

Took a step closer. And Luna didn't move.

Their eyes held for a moment longer, searching. Asking. Answering. Then Myra leaned in, just slightly, and Luna met her halfway.

The air thickened.

Neither of them moved fast. There was no dramatic pull, no hurried breath. Just a slow gravity pulling them into each other.

Myra tilted her head, her eyes searching Luna's one last time for any reason not to. But Luna was already leaning in, her lips parted in invitation.

Their mouths met in the gentlest collision: soft, patient, deliberate. It wasn't hungry. It wasn't meant to prove anything. It was reassurance, the kind of kiss that lingers more in the chest than on the lips.

Myra's hand rose, almost uncertainly, to Luna's waist, while Luna's fingers brushed the back of Myra's neck—light as a question, steady as a yes.

Their lips moved in quiet rhythm, slow and thoughtful, as if they were relearning the shape of each other's affection.

When they finally parted, it was only by a breath, foreheads resting together, eyes still closed.

Neither spoke. They didn't have to. The kiss had said it all.

Chapter 18
Dreams, Daughters, and Disbelief

The kitchen in Luna's house was warm and inviting, the smell of garlic and herbs floating lazily through the air while a smooth R&B playlist pulsed low from the Bluetooth speaker.

Myra stood barefoot at the island, chopping vegetables with a concentration that was… intense for someone cutting zucchini.

"This is nice," Myra said, glancing around the kitchen, knife still in hand. "Very… Martha Stewart meets neo-soul brunch vibes. I feel like I should be wearing linen and emotional stability."

Luna snorted from the stove, glancing over her shoulder. "Don't let the apron fool you," she said, gesturing to the black-and-white striped fabric tied around her waist. "I'm just good at pretending to know what I'm doing."

"Well, you're convincing," Myra replied, holding up the diced onions like a trophy. "Look at me. I'm participating in a grown-up activity. What's next, Chef Luna?"

"Throw those in the pan and stir," Luna instructed, nodding toward the sizzling skillet on the counter. "And don't get too cocky. I'm still side-eyeing the way you hold that knife."

Myra rolled her eyes, laughing. "You know what? That's fine. I'll let my culinary art speak for itself once you taste these vegetables."

"Oh, we're calling them art now?" Luna teased, stepping beside her to reach for the seasoning rack. Their arms brushed. Neither of them moved away.

The rhythm of the kitchen settled into something quieter.

As the food began to simmer, Luna leaned back against the counter, spoon still in hand, watching Myra with a faint smile.

"I like this," she said softly.

Myra paused, looking up from the cutting board. "What? My amateur cooking? Because I'll have you know this right here is a chopped champion effort."

Luna shook her head, her smile widening just a little. "No. This. You. Me. Just… this."

Myra didn't say anything right away. She didn't need to. Instead, she leaned into the moment, brushing her hand along Luna's arm as she walked past to toss the scraps in the compost bin.

"Well," she called over her shoulder with a smirk, "don't get too used to it. I only cook for people I really like."

Her teasing expression softened as she met Luna's gaze. "I like it too," she said simply.

As they worked together, the conversation flowed like the simmering sauce on the stove: easy, unforced, and full of flavor. Luna set the table while Myra poured two glasses of red, their laughter echoing off the kitchen walls. The clink of their glasses felt like a soft punctuation to the ease between them.

"So," Myra began as they settled into their chairs, plates steaming with pasta and roasted vegetables. She twirled a forkful and eyed Luna with a playful tilt of her head. "What about you? You've heard all about my circus of a dating history, but I don't know much about yours."

Luna paused mid-bite, her fork hovering just inches from her mouth. "What do you want to know?" she asked, her tone casual, though her eyes held a flicker of caution.

Myra set her wine glass down and leaned in a bit. "Anything. Everything. I want to know what your life's been like. Who you've been with. Who broke your heart. Who made you feel something."

Luna let out a slow breath, her lips tugging into a wry smile. "Ah, now we're getting to the real questions," she said, her voice teasing but thoughtful. She took a long sip of wine, letting the question settle before answering. "Well… there was someone. A couple years ago."

Myra's brows lifted, curious but careful. "What happened?"

Luna placed her glass back down, fingertips tracing the rim. "Her name was Courtney. She was sweet. Kind. Quiet in that way that makes you lean in closer just to catch what she's thinking. Preacher's daughter, if you can believe it."

Myra blinked. "Really?"

"Yeah," Luna said, smiling at the memory with a faint sadness.

"And somehow, despite all that, she found her way to me."

Myra tilted her head, waiting.

"She taught me patience," Luna continued, her voice soft. "She didn't move fast. Everything was intentional: dates, touch, words. Loving her was like standing still and feeling the wind shift. You couldn't always see it, but you felt it. And for a while, that was enough."

Myra stayed quiet, letting the weight of those words settle.

"But?" she finally asked.

"Eh… but she finally asked me what we were doing," Luna said, twirling her fork slowly. "And I gave her the honest answer. I told her I wasn't sure where it was going, but I liked her. I liked us. I thought it could work."

She paused, her expression growing pensive. "The problem was, deep down, I think she was waiting for a man."

Myra frowned slightly. "What do you mean?"

Luna let out a breath, her voice steady but quieter now. "She didn't say it outright, but I could feel it. Like I was just… a phase for her. Something she had to get out of her system before she settled into the life she thought she was supposed to have."

Myra's heart tugged at the rawness in Luna's tone. "That must've been hard."

"It was," Luna admitted, her eyes locking with Myra's. "Because I gave her real love. Even if it was quiet. Even if it wasn't perfect. I was serious. But it taught me something important: I don't want to be someone's experiment or their rebellion. I want someone who chooses me fully, without hesitation. Not because it's convenient or new, but because it's right."

Myra didn't hesitate. She reached across the table, her hand gently covering Luna's. "You deserve that," she said softly, her voice unwavering. "And for what it's worth, that's exactly how I feel about you."

Luna blinked once, slowly. Her fingers curled around Myra's in return, holding on just enough. "Thank you," she said quietly. "That means more than you know."

The moment stretched not in silence, but in understanding.

The conversation shifted back to lighter topics as they finished their meal, laughter filling the room once again. Luna cleared the plates while Myra leaned against the counter, watching her with a small smile.

"You know," Myra said, her voice thoughtful, "I think you're more domestic than you give yourself credit for."

Luna laughed, shaking her head as she wiped down the counter.

"Don't get used to it. This is a special occasion."

"Well, I feel special," Myra teased, taking a slow sip of wine.

Luna turned, a playful glint in her eye. "Good. Because I'm not letting you go."

Myra paused, cheeks flushed, but her gaze didn't waver. "Good," she echoed. "Because I don't want you to."

The words lingered in the air, quiet but weighty. A silent agreement, with no need to overexplain.

Later that night, they curled up on Luna's couch, wrapped in a shared blanket with soft R&B playing low in the background. A bottle of wine rested on the coffee table, half full. The lights were dim, the house quiet except for the faint hum of the music and the occasional clink of their glasses.

Myra tucked her legs beneath her, body angled toward Luna, who was thumbing through the TV menu aimlessly.

"You know," Myra began, swirling her wine, "I've been meaning to tell you about this dream I used to have."

Luna looked over, interest piqued. "Oh? Do I get to be in it?"

Myra chuckled. "You might have been," she said softly. "It was one of those dreams that showed up again and again over the years. Always the same."

"Alright then, tell me. What happened?"

Myra took a breath, her voice low and thoughtful.

"It's this house, big and full of light. Two stories. You walk in and just feel safe, like you've been there before."

She paused, eyes soft with memory. "I'm in the kitchen, packing lunch for our daughter. She's got these huge curls and this wild, bright smile that could light up the block. She hugs me goodbye, and then she's out the door."

Luna leaned in slightly, saying nothing, letting the image settle.

Myra continued, slower now. "After she leaves, I go upstairs to get ready. And there's always this moment—me, standing in front of a mirror in our bedroom. Then arms wrap around me from behind. She presses her lips to my neck and whispers, 'Good morning.'"

A blush crept across Myra's cheeks. "I remember every detail. The white walls. Soft gray curtains. That light blue bedspread. It feels… calm. Like home."

Luna's gaze didn't waver. The room felt still.

"You've had this dream more than once?" she asked quietly.

Myra nodded. "More times than I can count. And it never changes. It feels less like a dream and more like a memory that hasn't happened yet."

Luna set her glass down, fingers brushing the stem a little too long. "That's wild," she whispered. "Because I've had the same dream."

Myra's eyes widened. "You're serious?"

"Dead serious," Luna said, her voice low and steady. "Same room. Same bedspread. White walls. But I never see the woman's face. Just this little girl with curly hair, bursting into the room saying, 'Mommy, wake up! Me and Mommy made breakfast!'"

Myra's breath caught in her throat. "You're not playing?"

Luna shook her head slowly. "The first time, I thought it was nothing. But it came back, again and again. And every time, it felt like it meant something I couldn't explain."

Myra stared at her, the space between them suddenly feeling like fate itself. "You really think it's not just coincidence?"

"I don't know," Luna murmured, "but hearing you say it like that... it felt like you just filled in all the pieces I never had words for."

Myra smiled gently, reaching for her hand. "It doesn't sound strange to me. It sounds... right."

Luna laced their fingers together. "Maybe it's not just a dream," she said quietly. "Maybe it's a vision of what we're meant to build."

Myra's heart swelled. Her voice was barely above a whisper. "You believe that?"

"I do," Luna replied. "And for once... I'm not afraid. I'm not afraid of us."

Myra leaned in just a little, their foreheads nearly touching.

"Neither am I."

They sat in comfortable silence for a while, their hands still linked, the weight of their shared dreams settling over them like a blanket. For the first time in a long time, it felt like the future wasn't something to fear but something to look forward to.

As the warmth of their conversation lingered, Myra's phone buzzed on the coffee table. She glanced at the screen, and her stomach dropped when she saw the name: Jordan. Another message followed, then another.

Luna noticed Myra's subtle change in expression. Her brow furrowed as she leaned forward. "Who's that?" she asked, her tone cautious but sharp.

Myra hesitated, her fingers brushing against her phone before she finally turned the screen over. "It's Jordan," she admitted quietly.

Luna's jaw tightened. "Have you seen her recently?"

Myra let out a long sigh, her hand instinctively running through her hair. "No, I haven't," she replied honestly. "But we've exchanged a few texts."

Luna's eyes narrowed. "Why? What could you possibly have left to say to her?"

Myra felt her chest tighten, the weight of the unspoken truths between them pressing down hard. She debated whether to finally spill her secret or keep dancing around it. The silence stretched.

Myra's phone buzzed again, lighting up on the coffee table.

Another message from Jordan.

Luna didn't miss the way Myra's eyes flickered toward it—hesitant, guilty, familiar. "That her again?" Luna asked, her voice low but already coiled tight.

Myra didn't answer immediately. She reached for the phone, thumb hovering over the screen, then set it back down like it burned. "Yeah."

Luna stood up slowly. "Let me guess, she wants to know if being with me is worth what you lost with her?"

Myra flinched. "Something like that."

Luna scoffed, pacing now. "I don't get it. Why is she even still texting you, Myra? Why is she still in the picture at all?"

"I haven't been responding," Myra said quickly. "I haven't been feeding into it."

"But she thinks she still has a lane," Luna snapped. "And the only reason she thinks that is because you left one open."

Myra stood too, her voice rising. "It's not like that. She's just trying to process—"

"Oh, don't you dare," Luna interrupted, fire behind her eyes.

"Don't you dare defend her. She's not the one who walked out on me with no warning. She's not the one who ghosted her best friend like I was just some phase you outgrew."

Myra's mouth parted. "Luna—"

"No!" Luna cut in, her voice cracking. "You don't get to smooth this over. You left, Myra. No text. No explanation. Just gone. And the worst part? I thought I did something wrong. I kept replaying everything in my head, like: Did I say too much? Was I too close? Did I push too hard?"

Myra's eyes welled, her voice barely audible. "You didn't do anything wrong."

"But I didn't know that!" Luna shouted. "Because you never told me. You just left. I was in love with you, and I thought I was crazy for it."

Myra froze. "You were what?"

Luna's chest heaved. "In. Love. With. You. And I said nothing because I thought maybe, just maybe, you didn't feel the same. But then you left, and not just for anyone, you left for her. And I knew, I knew she wasn't right for you. But I had to sit there and watch you try and build something with someone who didn't even see you."

Myra stepped closer, her voice trembling. "I did feel the same. I've loved you for a long time, Luna."

"Then why didn't you say it?" Luna demanded, tears slipping down her cheeks now. "Why didn't you just open your mouth and say it before everything fell apart?"

"Because I was scared," Myra said, her voice breaking. "You were my person. My anchor. I thought if I told you how I felt and you didn't feel it back, I'd lose you. I didn't think I could survive that."

"So instead, you disappeared and left me to deal with the loss anyway," Luna whispered. "You broke me in silence, Myra."

Myra reached for her hand, but Luna pulled away.

"And Nicole?" Luna said bitterly. "That was who you chose over me?"

Myra let out a shaky breath. "I didn't choose her. I chose the idea of running. I chose distraction. And I paid for it. You were right. She wasn't really gay. She wanted to play house with me until she got tired and went back to what was safe."

Luna looked at her, raw pain etched into every line of her face. "So while I was here, wondering what I did wrong, you were with someone who made you question your worth. That didn't have to happen, Myra. None of this did."

Myra stepped forward again, slower this time. "You're right. It didn't. But I let fear drive every decision. And I'm sorry. Not just for what I did, but for everything I didn't say when it mattered."

Luna stood there, trembling from the weight of everything they'd finally said aloud. Then she yelled, "I needed you. And you weren't there!"

"I didn't know better," Myra snapped, her voice cracking under pressure. "I was confused and scared, Luna. I didn't know how to handle what I was feeling. So yeah, I made the wrong choice. But I'm here now, telling the truth. Owning it."

"Too late," Luna shot back, her voice icy. She stepped forward, her eyes dark and blazing. "Do you have any idea what that did to me? Watching you walk away like none of it meant anything, like I didn't mean anything, only to see you crash and burn just like I knew you would?"

Myra flinched at her words, guilt rising like bile in her throat. "You don't think I've punished myself for that every single day?" she said, her voice trembling. "I know I hurt you. I know I destroyed everything we had. But I didn't know how to stay."

Luna let out a bitter, humorless laugh. "Staying would've been the easiest thing, Myra. Staying meant choosing me. Trusting me. Trusting us. But no, you ran. You left me in the dark to go play house with someone who didn't even know what to do with you."

Myra's fists clenched at her sides. "I'm not proud of it, Luna. I'm not standing here asking you to pretend it didn't happen. But I can't rewrite it. I can only give you the truth now."

Luna's voice sharpened like a blade. "The truth? You mean now you want to tell the truth? When it's convenient for you? You think I'm supposed to be grateful you finally grew a conscience?"

She started pacing, her hands flying to her hair like she was trying to physically shake off the years she had kept quiet. "You didn't trust me enough to tell me the truth, Myra. You didn't give me a chance to be there for you. Instead, you left, and I was stuck trying to figure out what the hell I did wrong while you played soulmate with someone who never saw you."

Myra's tears spilled fast now. "You don't think I already know that? You don't think I've lived with that every single day? I broke us. I ruined everything. But I didn't know how to fix it. I still don't."

Luna stopped pacing, fury simmering in her voice. "So now what? You show up, say you're sorry, and I'm supposed to what, forget everything you put me through? Pretend I didn't spend years wondering what I did wrong to make you leave me behind?"

Myra stepped back, her voice softer but still wrecked. "No. I don't expect that. I just… I needed you to know. I couldn't keep pretending you didn't deserve the truth."

Luna's jaw tightened, her entire body tense. "I didn't just deserve the truth. I deserved a choice. You took that from me. You decided for me. And now you want to cry about how you didn't think I'd want you once you were broken?"

Myra's voice cracked as she whispered, "I didn't think you'd want someone so messed up. Someone who left."

"That wasn't your decision to make," Luna snapped. "That was my decision. You robbed me of that. And you want to talk about how you've loved me this whole time?"

Silence.

Heavy. Dense. Final.

"I should go," Myra said quietly, her voice raw and shaking. Luna didn't move. She didn't look at her. Her arms stayed crossed, her gaze pinned to the floor.

"Yeah," she muttered, cold and distant. "Maybe you should."

Myra's hand tightened around the doorknob. She paused, turning slightly as her eyes searched Luna's face—hoping, praying—for some flicker of softness, something to tell her this wasn't the end. But all she saw was steel. Anger layered over hurt, vulnerability buried too deep to reach. Luna's expression didn't change.

With a quiet breath, Myra turned back to the door. Each step felt heavier than the last. At the threshold, she glanced over her shoulder one last time.

"I'm sorry, Luna," she whispered, her voice cracking. "For everything."

Luna's lip twitched like she might speak. Her throat moved, her eyes flicking toward Myra's—but just as quickly, she looked away.

She said nothing.

The door clicked shut. And she was alone.

Luna stood frozen, staring at nothing. Her eyes landed on a photo frame across the room, but her gaze slid through it like glass.

Slowly, her arms uncrossed. Her hands curled into trembling fists at her sides. The room was silent. But inside her, the storm still raged.

She let out a breath that trembled on its way out and whispered into the empty space, barely holding back the ache:

"You don't get to walk in here, break me open, and make me wonder if you'll walk out again."

Chapter 19
Echoes and Absences

Luna sat in her parked car outside the studio, engine running but unmoved. She'd been there for twelve minutes. Her coffee had gone cold in the cupholder, untouched. A half-finished voice note to her assistant blinked on her phone screen, but she couldn't bring herself to hit send.

She wasn't ready to talk. Not about branding. Not about the new pitch deck. Not about her. Not yet.

The argument with Myra still clung to her skin like heat after a fever, Myra's voice still echoing in her ears:

You don't get to walk in here, break me open, and make me wonder if you'll walk out again.

She meant it. She really did. But she hadn't slept last night either.

With a sigh that scraped her throat, Luna finally killed the ignition and stepped out of the car. The morning air was humid, sticky like guilt, and even her usual walk into the building felt heavier than usual. Her steps lacked rhythm. The bounce in her stride was gone. Her sharpness dulled.

Inside, her team was already buzzing. Camera gear being prepped. Someone laughing over a TikTok in the corner. Coffee brewing. But to Luna, it all sounded like white noise.

"Morning, Luna," one of the interns chirped brightly.

Luna forced a half-smile. "Morning," she said, but it felt like someone else's voice coming out of her mouth.

She dropped her bag in her office, closed the door behind her, and stared at her reflection in the glass wall. Her eyes were tired. Not from lack of sleep, but from emotional whiplash.

She'd spent five years building walls to forget Myra. One dinner and a few dreams later, they were rubble.

She slumped into her chair, eyes flicking to her phone. No missed calls. No texts. She didn't know whether to feel relieved or abandoned.

And that pissed her off.

Because how dare Myra still have that kind of hold on her. How dare she speak about love like it was something you just circle back to when you're ready. As if she hadn't been the one left in silence. As if she hadn't spent nights wondering what she did wrong.

Luna pulled up her Google Calendar, trying to distract herself. But even the client names blurred together. All she could hear was Myra's voice:

I didn't think you'd want someone so messed up.

Her hands curled into fists before she even realized it.

She opened her journal file instead. She hadn't touched it in weeks. But today, she typed:

I'm angry.

Not just at her. At myself.

For still wanting to believe her.

The cursor blinked at her like it was waiting for more, but she didn't have it in her. Not today.

She closed the laptop and pressed the heels of her hands to her eyes, grounding herself. She didn't have the luxury of spiraling. Not this week.

Not with the talk show interview coming up.

Her eyes flicked toward the garment bag hanging on the coat rack, the outfit already steamed and styled. She had a pre-interview prep call in an hour, a press run starting tomorrow, and a segment scheduled to air nationally by the end of the week.

This was supposed to be her season.

And she couldn't afford to look like someone barely keeping it together.

As Luna arrived to her interview dressing room, she rolled her shoulders back, and walked over to the mirror. Her reflection stared back at her—disheveled, but still standing. She grabbed her edge control and brush from the drawer, pulling her baby hairs into place with the kind of precision only a woman used to covering up pain could manage.

Lip gloss. Concealer. Liner. Mask on.

. . . .

A thousand moments later, Luna sat across from the camera, her reflection now broadcast for everyone to see.

"Luna Cain, founder of Cain Studios, welcome back to the show. You've been called the 'Visual Voice of a Generation.' How does that feel?"

She nodded once and said aloud, "It feels like a lot of pressure. But it also feels like purpose."

Her voice didn't crack this time. She'd show up.

Even if part of her heart was still tangled in the sound of Myra's apology.

A few weeks later, Luna sat at her desk, the soft click of her keyboard the only sound in the room as she skimmed a calendar of upcoming speaking engagements and events. Her office buzzed faintly outside the door: emails flying, deadlines looming. Inside, everything was calm and in control.

Until Nikki appeared.

Her assistant knocked lightly on the open door, then stepped inside holding a massive bouquet of white roses and sprigs of soft lavender. The scent wafted in ahead of her, instantly changing the room's energy.

"Uh, these just arrived for you," Nikki said, grinning as she set the arrangement down. "Smells expensive."

Luna glanced at the flowers, her face unreadable. "Who sent them?"

"There's a card," Nikki added, lifting her brows like she already knew the answer. "Want me to read it?"

"No," Luna said too quickly, reaching for the card before Nikki could even think about it.

She slipped the small envelope open with practiced fingers and scanned the familiar handwriting.

Luna,
Congratulations on all your success.
You deserve every bit of it.
– Myra

Her heart didn't race, but it did pause.

She didn't smile. Didn't frown. Just pressed her lips into a flat line as her fingers hovered over the note. She didn't tear it up. Didn't tuck it away somewhere private. She slid it neatly back into the envelope and pushed it under a small stack of folders— just enough to hide it, not enough to forget it.

"Well?" Nikki probed, arms crossed now. "Are we pretending that's from a brand collaboration or…?"

Luna looked up slowly, her tone flat. "It's not a secret admirer."

"So it is someone who knows you." Nikki's tone was feather-light, but her eyes were sharp.

"Just someone being polite."

Nikki gave a knowing smile. "Uh-huh. The polite kind that knows your favorite flowers? That polite?"

Luna's eyes flicked back to the bouquet. White roses. Lavender.

Softness. Clarity. Myra knew that. Myra remembered.

"I already know what they're trying to say," she said quietly, turning her attention back to her screen. "And it doesn't change anything."

Nikki's voice softened, stepping out of assistant mode for a moment. "You know, it's okay to want it to mean something."

Luna didn't look up. "Let's just keep this professional."

Nikki sighed but didn't press. "Alright, boss. But for the record? They're beautiful."

As the door clicked shut behind her, Luna leaned back in her chair, staring at the arrangement again. The scent curled around her like a memory. Her chest tightened.

She hated how Myra still knew exactly where to touch, even from a distance.

That evening, the glow of the television flickered across Luna's dimly lit living room. She sat curled up on the corner of her velvet couch, wrapped in an oversized knit throw, a half-finished glass of red wine resting on the side table. The remote dangled loosely in her hand as she flipped through channel after channel, not really watching, just filling the silence.

She stopped when she recognized herself.

A rerun of the talk show she'd appeared on earlier in the week lit up the screen. There she was: polished, composed, answering questions with grace and quiet charisma. Her blazer was crisp, her smile effortless, her voice steady as she spoke about her journey, her vision, her rising platform.

But from where she sat now, that version of her felt distant, like a highlight reel from someone else's life.

The camera panned in on her on-screen self laughing, hands folded in her lap, talking about staying true to yourself in a world that wants to box you in.

Luna let out a soft, ironic breath. If only it were that simple. Her phone buzzed beside her on the cushion. She glanced down.

Myra: *Miss you. Just wanted to say I'm proud of you.*

The words sat there glowing in the low light, small and unassuming, but they hit like a gut punch.

Luna stared at the screen, her thumb hovering just above the message. The instinct to reply was immediate, primal. Just a few words. A door cracked open. A moment of softness.

But then she heard it, Myra's voice in her memory, trembling during their fight: "I didn't know how to stay."

Her jaw tensed.

The flowers. The note. Now this.

She locked the phone and set it down gently but deliberately on the edge of the coffee table.

Leaning back against the cushions, Luna exhaled and closed her eyes. The soft hum of the television filled the room. Her reflection still played on the screen, speaking about empowerment and healing and owning your truth.

But tonight, the truth was simple:

She wasn't ready to forgive. Not yet.

And Myra's absence, no matter how loudly it echoed, would not rush her healing.

CHAPTER 20
STEPS TOWARD MAYBE

Myra lounged on the plush sectional in her new expansive living room, a glass of red wine cradled in her hand. The modern space—high ceilings, polished concrete floors, warm wood tones, and subtle gold accents—usually made her feel accomplished. Safe. Like she'd finally arrived somewhere that mattered.

But tonight, it felt too still. Too curated. Too quiet.

The television cast soft, rhythmic flashes across the room, painting her face in alternating hues of light and shadow. Onscreen, Luna sat in front of a sleek talk show set, all poise and brilliance. Her voice floated through the speakers: articulate, composed, magnetic. Her laugh, the way she tilted her head when speaking, how her hands moved just slightly when she was passionate about something—it all felt achingly familiar.

Myra didn't even notice she was smiling until the voice snapped her out of it.

"Still obsessed, huh?"

Jayy's teasing tone broke the trance.

She glanced up, watching him stroll in from the kitchen, casual as ever. A six-pack of craft beer dangled from one hand, a crinkled bag of chips from the other. He dropped onto the couch like he owned the place.

"I'm not obsessed," Myra said, shifting in her seat as she took another sip. "I'm… interested."

Jayy snorted. "Interested enough to have this thing recorded, queued, and played on loop like it's the Super Bowl halftime show?"

She threw a pillow at him. "You're the worst."

"And yet you keep inviting me over," he said with a smirk, catching the pillow mid-air. "So? Any response yet? She still giving you silence?"

Myra's face softened, her eyes drifting back to the screen. Luna was answering a question about creative identity, and the way she spoke made Myra's chest tighten.

"Yeah," she murmured. "No texts. No calls. Nothing."

Jayy shook his head. "Damn. Not even a 'thanks for the flowers'? That's cold."

"She's hurt, Jayy," Myra replied, her voice low. "And it's not like she doesn't have a reason to be. I left her in the dark. I never gave her a real chance."

He studied her for a moment, then reached into the chip bag and tossed one into his mouth. "Look, you did what most people don't: owned your shit. You showed up. You told her the truth. You even sent the flowers and that corny-ass card."

Myra managed a faint smile. "You helped me write that card, by the way."

"Exactly, which is why I know it was corny," he said, nudging her. "But it was honest. And that's the part that matters."

Myra leaned her head back against the couch, staring up at the ceiling like it might hold some answers. "I don't know what I expected. Maybe a door cracked open. A chance."

"Maybe she just needs time," Jayy said, his tone gentler now. "You broke her open, Mai. Sometimes that kind of thing doesn't heal overnight."

Myra closed her eyes, the warmth of the wine lingering on her tongue, the ache in her chest refusing to budge. "Yeah," she whispered. "But what if I waited too long?"

Jayy didn't answer. He didn't have to.

The TV flickered in front of them, Luna's face still glowing in the frame. Poised. Brilliant. Unreachable.

And Myra sat in silence, her heart resting somewhere in the quiet between what could've been and what still might be.

Jayy nudged her with his elbow, breaking the weight in the room with a shift in energy. "Speaking of doing what you can, what's this big party I keep hearing about? You've been working your ass off for this moment."

Myra sat up a little straighter, the tension in her shoulders easing. "My company hit Millionaire Gold Status last month," she said, a glimmer of pride warming her voice. "It's a huge milestone, first time hitting that number. So I'm throwing a celebration here: catered, live music, everyone who's anyone in the industry will be there."

Jayy gave a low whistle and lifted his beer in salute. "Look at you, Ms. Boss Lady. You deserve this. To hard work paying off."

Myra raised her wine glass, tapping it gently against his bottle.

"To hard work."

They sipped in silence for a moment, the sound of Luna's interview still playing softly in the background like a memory that refused to fade.

Jayy leaned back, his tone more casual now. "So… you inviting her?"

Myra froze mid-sip, the stem of her glass caught between her fingers. "You think I should?"

He shot her a look. "I think you're going to, whether I say yes or no. You're not exactly subtle when it comes to Luna."

Myra exhaled a soft laugh, placing her glass down and reaching for her phone on the coffee table. "You know me too well."

Jayy smiled, but his eyes were kind. "Maybe she shows up. Maybe she doesn't. Either way, you did the work—for the company, for yourself. You're showing up for you now, and that matters more than anything."

Myra glanced at the screen one more time, Luna's voice fading out as the interview cut to commercial.

She opened her messages, hesitating over Luna's name, her thumb hovering once again above the screen.

Myra scrolled to Luna's thread, the silence between them laid bare in the absence of blue bubbles. The lack of recent replies stared back at her, quiet but heavy. Her fingers hovered over the keyboard for a moment before she started typing:

Hey Luna,

I know things have been tense between us lately, but I wanted to invite you to my company's Millionaire Gold Status celebration party. It's this Friday at my house. It'd mean a lot to me if you came.

She stared at the message, her thumb trembling slightly above the send button.

"What if she doesn't come?" Myra asked quietly, not really looking at Jayy.

He leaned back, arms stretched across the back of the couch. "Then that's her loss. But if she does… maybe it's a step in the right direction."

Myra drew in a slow breath and pressed send. The message disappeared, delivered into the unknown. She set the phone down gently and picked up her wine glass again, trying to soothe the anxious flutter tightening her chest.

"It's out of my hands now," she murmured.

Jayy gave her a nod, his voice easy but genuine. "Either way, this party's going to be epic. You've built something incredible, Myra. Luna or no Luna, you've got a lot to celebrate."

Myra smiled faintly, but her mind stayed tangled in the past and the possibility of what might still come.

As Jayy turned his attention to the TV, Myra let her gaze drift toward the soft hum of the screen. She thought of Luna's laugh, her eyes, the fire in her voice. And for a moment, she let herself wonder.

Maybe this party wasn't just a celebration of what she'd built.

Maybe it could be the start of something she still hoped to rebuild.

CHAPTER 21
THE INVITATION

Luna's mornings ran like clockwork.

Her day began with a predawn workout in the apartment gym, the rhythmic thud of her sneakers against the treadmill breaking the quiet. A long, steam-heavy shower followed, fogging the mirror until her reflection was nothing more than a ghostly outline. Fresh coffee filled her favorite black mug, always placed to the right of her laptop before she headed out.

By the time she unlocked her office doors, the building was still settling into the morning. The sharp click of Nikki's heels echoed across the polished floor, announcing her arrival before she appeared in the doorway, a stack of event proposals tucked under her arm.

"Don't forget about the client brunch at noon," she said, setting them on the desk with a tidy little pat.

"Got it," Luna replied, scanning the top sheet.

Her phone buzzed next to her coffee mug. She didn't have to look to know who it was. But she did anyway. Hey Luna, I know things have been tense between us lately, but I wanted to invite you to my company's Millionaire Gold Status celebration party. It's this Friday at my house. It'd mean a lot to me if you came.

Hope you're doing well.

Myra.

Her eyes traced the words once, twice. The ache bloomed in her chest before she could stop it that instinctive pull toward Myra, the part of her that still wanted to close the space between them. But memory rushed in just as quick: raised voices, sharp silences, the heaviness that followed her home that night.

Don't go there.

She locked the phone and placed it face down, pressing her fingertips to the desk like she could root herself to the present.

The week unfolded in a blur of motion.

Monday's shoot. Tuesday's investor call. Wednesday's back-to- back consultations. She stacked her days so tight there was barely space to think but still, Myra's name clung to the edges of her mind.

On Tuesday, during a strategy meeting, Nikki caught her staring past the screen at the skyline. "Do you want me to run through that part again?" she asked, pausing mid- sentence.

Luna blinked, forcing herself back into the room. "No. I'm following." Nikki tilted her head. "Following doesn't always mean listening."

A corner of Luna's mouth lifted, but it didn't reach her eyes. "I'm fine."

"Uh-huh." Nikki slid the presentation to the next slide but didn't let it go. "You know, I've worked for you long enough to know when your mind's in two places at once."

Only two? Luna thought, but she kept that to herself.

By Wednesday's shoot, Nikki had stopped skirting around it. She set a bottle of water in front of Luna and leaned on the table. "Alright, spill. You've been… different this week. You're working, but your spark's on low."

"I don't have a spark. I have deadlines."

"Don't play me." Nikki's eyes softened, but she didn't break the line of sight. "You got a message, didn't you?"

Luna froze for half a second, just long enough for Nikki to see it.

"Look," Nikki said, lowering her voice, "I'm not telling you to do anything about it. But bottling it up? That's not you."

It is now, Luna thought. Aloud, she said, "Some things are better left alone."

"Or," Nikki countered, "some things just need time."

Luna glanced at her phone—still dark, still untouched—and forced herself to refocus on the photographer giving instructions.

The rest of the week played out the same. Polished answers. Controlled smiles. Flawless execution. But between tasks, her mind slipped. She'd find herself scrolling through her camera roll and stopping on an old photo before snapping out of it. Or staring at her phone just long enough to wonder if she should reply.

Every time, she chose not to.

By Friday afternoon, Nikki leaned against the doorframe of Luna's office, arms crossed. "So… are we going or not?"

Luna didn't look up from her laptop. "We?"

"You know what I mean." Nikki stepped inside, dropping a glossy folder on the desk. "Myra's party. You've been pretending you're not thinking about it all week, but I can practically hear the mental tug-of-war from here.

Luna's fingers paused on the keyboard. "It's not that simple."

"Sure it is. You either go or you don't. What's the worst that happens? You say hi, eat free food, and leave?"

Luna leaned back in her chair, exhaling slowly. "The worst that happens is I walk into her world again and forget why I walked out of it in the first place."

Nikki's expression softened. "Or… the best that happens is you find some clarity. Either way, hiding from it won't make it go away."

For a moment, the only sound in the room was the faint hum of the city outside the window. Luna finally closed her laptop. "Fine. I'll go. But only because I need to get you off my back."

"Mm-hmm." Nikki smirked, clearly unconvinced. "I'll text you the address so you can't 'accidentally' forget."

Later that evening, Luna stood in front of her bedroom mirror, assessing her reflection like she was preparing for a press interview. A fitted black suit hugged her frame, sharp and elegant. She smoothed a hand over the fabric, then reached for the gold hoops Myra had once called her "power earrings."

She hesitated, holding them in her palm. *Why am I even thinking about what she'd notice?*

Still, she put them on.

The faint scent of her favorite perfume filled the air as she gave herself one last look. Outwardly, she looked every bit the composed, untouchable woman she'd worked so hard to be. Inwardly, her thoughts were a quiet storm: questions she couldn't silence, memories she couldn't erase.

She grabbed her clutch and keys, telling herself it was just another event. Just another night.

But deep down, she knew it wasn't.

By the time she pulled up to Myra's driveway, Luna had her expression locked in place, a quiet, self-assured mask that gave nothing away. She stepped out of the car, the muted thump of bass from inside syncing with her heartbeat.

The front doors opened, and the hum of conversation seemed to thin for just a second, like the house itself noticed.

Luna stepped inside.

She wasn't overdressed, but somehow every detail felt deliberate: the tailored black suit jacket with silk lapels, the deep V-neck blouse that caught the light just enough, the glint of gold at her ears. Her hair framed her face in soft waves, the kind that looked both effortless and impossible to replicate. She scanned the room, not in a way that demanded attention, but in a way that made the attention find her anyway.

Myra's eyes found her instantly, and the familiar ache bloomed before she could stop it. The air between them stretched thin when Luna's gaze swept across the room and landed on her. For the briefest moment, their eyes locked, an unspoken recognition, a ghost of what they used to be.

Myra smiled. Small, warm. Not too much, but enough to say I see you.

And Luna, after the slightest pause, gave the faintest curve of her lips in return before shifting her focus elsewhere.

Before Myra could think to move toward her, Jayy was already there, cutting across the room with that unbothered stride he had. He clasped Luna into a quick hug, the two exchanging easy banter like old friends. Jayy said something that made Luna throw her head back and laugh, and Myra felt the sound like a tug at her ribcage.

Then Luna was gone, melting into the crowd like she'd been here all along. She spoke with a small group near the art wall, then drifted toward the bar, effortlessly slipping into conversation with someone Myra recognized from a past industry event. She mingled like she belonged because she did.

Myra lingered where she was, pretending to be absorbed in the conversation at her side, but every few minutes her gaze flicked back to where Luna moved through the room. She didn't go over. Not yet. She wasn't ready.

As Myra moved through the crowd, shaking hands and exchanging pleasantries, she sipped at her champagne just enough to keep it from getting warm. She was mid-conversation with a pair of investors when movement at the bar caught her eye.

Luna.

She was leaning against the counter, one elbow resting casually, laughing with someone Myra vaguely recognized from the industry. That laugh—unforced, easy—carried just enough over the crowd to curl in Myra's chest. She tried not to stare, but her eyes tracked her anyway.

Luna reached into her clutch for her phone, pulling it free with a smooth flick of her wrist. The clutch tipped slightly on its side as she spoke, her attention locked on the person in front of her. Myra's gaze dipped just long enough to catch the dull metallic glint of keys sliding free and landing softly against the polished bar.

Luna didn't notice.

Myra excused herself from the investors with a smile she didn't quite mean. She slipped between two guests, brushing past a waiter carrying a tray of hors d'oeuvres, and reached the bar just as the keys threatened to slide further toward the edge.

Her fingers closed around them before they could hit the floor. Cool metal, a small keychain she instantly recognized—Luna's initials in sleek silver letters.

She could have tapped her on the shoulder. Could have said, *Hey, you dropped these.*

But Luna was walking and talking still mid-conversation, still wearing that effortless smile, and something in Myra's chest clenched at the thought of walking up and interrupting like any other stranger.

So instead, she tucked the keys into her palm, letting them disappear into the folds of her pocket. I'll give them back later, she told herself, though she wasn't entirely sure if "later" meant tonight, or somewhere quieter, somewhere without an audience.

The crowd swallowed her again, and as she moved back toward the center of the room, the weight of the keys against her leg felt heavier than it should have, like a secret she wasn't ready to let go of.

Myra floated from group to group, champagne flute in hand, her smile effortlessly charming. She was halfway through a conversation with a pair of investors when she noticed Luna across the room, speaking with one of their old mutuals. For a moment, their eyes almost met—almost—before Myra looked away, keeping her composure.

That's when she heard it.

A voice she knew too well, cutting through the din. "Wow. This is… something."

Myra's spine went rigid. Slowly, she turned toward the foyer. And there was Jordan, standing just inside, looking like she'd been plucked from another lifetime. The crowd hadn't quite registered her yet, but Myra had.

"What are you doing here?" Myra's voice was low but sharp as she stepped away from her guests, closing the distance.

Jordan's smirk was the same as it had always been: equal parts charm and provocation. "I heard about your big night. Thought I'd come congratulate you."

"This isn't the time," Myra said, forcing a calm she didn't feel. "Funny, you never seemed to mind when I showed up before."

The exchange was quiet enough that only the people closest could catch it, but Myra saw movement at the edge of the room: Luna, now watching from across the way, her expression unreadable.

Myra took a breath, tilting her head toward the door. "You need to leave, Jordan. Tonight isn't about you."

Jordan's smirk faltered, just slightly. "You haven't changed." "And you haven't grown up," Myra shot back.

For a moment, neither moved. Then Jordan gave a humorless laugh and stepped backward toward the door. "Enjoy your party."

The front door clicked shut behind her, but the disruption lingered. Myra stood there for a beat, feeling the weight of every pair of eyes, including Luna's. She smoothed the fabric of her clothing, pasted on her smile, and turned back to her guests as if nothing had happened.

The murmur of conversation swelled again as the front door closed behind Jordan. Myra stood still for a beat, wine glass in hand, the echo of their exchange still humming in her ears. She caught Jayy's eye across the room, his raised brow silently asking if she was okay. She gave him a small nod—barely there—before straightening her shoulders.

No one else needed to know. Not tonight.

She stepped toward the small stage area set up in the corner of the living room, the soft wash of uplighting casting her in gold.

A gentle tap on her glass drew the crowd's attention, and within moments the music lowered, voices quieting.

"First off," she began, her tone warm but steady, "thank you all for being here tonight. This"—she gestured around at the bustling, glittering room—"is more than just a party. It's a celebration of hard work, long nights, and believing in something even when no one else could see it yet."

Her gaze swept the room, pausing just for a breath when it landed on Luna.

"This year, my company reached Millionaire Gold Status. And I say 'my company,' but really, it's our success. The people who've supported me, collaborated with me, challenged me… you're the reason we're here."

A ripple of applause moved through the guests. Myra smiled, but there was a flicker in her eyes, something softer, something only a few might catch.

"Tonight is about more than numbers," she continued. "It's about the people who've walked beside you on the journey. The ones who've shown up. And the ones who inspire you to keep going, whether they're right here by your side or just… here." She tapped her chest lightly.

She raised her glass. "To growth. To grit. To every single one of you. Cheers."

The room erupted into clinking glasses and laughter as the music swelled again. Myra stepped down from the platform, her smile still in place, but her mind had already drifted, drawn like a magnet to the brief moment during her speech when her eyes met Luna's.

She eased back into the crowd, accepting quick congratulations and handshakes along the way, her responses automatic. The earlier confrontation still hummed faintly in her chest, but it was the sight across the room that truly stole her focus.

There was Luna, bathed in the soft golden light, her profile framed by the curve of her jaw as she tilted her head in polite laughter at something their mutual acquaintance was saying.

Myra started toward her, weaving between guests, but a hand on her arm stopped her.

"Myra! I need you to meet someone," one of her colleagues said, pulling her toward a group of out-of-town investors.

She stole a glance over her shoulder. Luna was still there, but now speaking to someone else.

A few minutes later, she tried again, excusing herself and slipping through the crowd. She was almost there when her event planner intercepted her with a clipboard. "The catering team needs your approval on the dessert presentation."

Myra nodded distractedly, signing off as fast as she could, but by the time she looked back, Luna had moved toward the patio.

On the third attempt, she finally caught sight of Luna near the bar. Myra stepped forward, only for a tipsy guest to stumble into her path, launching into an enthusiastic monologue about the real estate market. Myra's polite laugh hid her growing impatience, her eyes darting past the guest's shoulder, locking on Luna's once more.

But then someone else leaned in to talk to Luna, blocking her from view entirely.

Myra exhaled through her nose, the champagne flute in her hand suddenly feeling heavier. It was like the universe was conspiring to keep them apart.

The next half hour blurred into a steady current of handshakes, posed photos, and toasts. Myra drifted between clusters of guests, smiling for cameras and thanking investors, all the while keeping half an eye on the crowd for a glimpse of her.

Across the room, Luna had found herself in her own orbit. She chatted briefly with the live band's lead singer about a potential collaboration, then accepted a fresh glass of wine from one of the caterers making their rounds. She lingered near the art installation Myra had commissioned for the evening, a sleek gold structure in the shape of a key, but she never crossed into Myra's immediate circle.

That's when Jayy spotted her.

"Well, well, well," he drawled, appearing at her side like he'd been waiting for this moment all night. "Look who decided to stick around instead of ghosting early."

Luna smirked over the rim of her wine glass. "What, you keeping tabs on me now?"

"Please," Jayy scoffed, glancing around at the crowd. "You're hard to miss. Myra's party, you standing in the shadows like some VIP with a secret agenda. Makes a man curious."

"I don't do agendas," she said smoothly, though her eyes betrayed the smallest flicker toward the far side of the room, where Myra was laughing with a group of colleagues.

Jayy caught it instantly. "Mm-hmm. Right. And I'm just here for the free food."

Luna chuckled despite herself, shaking her head. "You're ridiculous."

"And you," Jayy said, taking a slow sip of his beer, "are still avoiding her."

"I'm not avoiding," Luna replied, her tone a touch too quick.

"Uh-huh. You're strategically repositioning yourself in the opposite direction every time she's within ten feet," Jayy teased. "Don't worry. I won't tell her. Yet."

Luna gave him a look, half warning and half amused. "Don't you have people to charm?"

"I'm charming you right now," he shot back, before tipping his beer in her direction and strolling off into the crowd.

She watched him go, a reluctant smile tugging at her lips, though it faded as her eyes found Myra again across the room. The crowd had thinned, the music softened into a mellow hum, and conversations floated in quieter pockets. Empty champagne flutes and half-eaten plates dotted the tables, signs that the night was winding down.

Jayy reappeared with two glasses of sparkling water, plopping down beside her on the couch like they'd been doing this every Saturday night for years. "Not bad for a rich-people party," he teased, handing her a glass.

"Not bad," Luna said, taking it.

They fell into easy conversation, dissecting the fashion choices of the evening and laughing about a tipsy guest who had cornered Jayy to pitch an "unbeatable" business idea involving glow-in-the-dark yoga mats. But every now and then, Luna's gaze wandered, searching almost involuntarily, for Myra.

Eventually, she leaned back and set her glass on the low table. "Alright, I should head out before I'm roped into cleaning up," she said with a smirk. She reached into her bag. Her fingers paused, then searched again.

Jayy noticed. "What?"

"My keys," she said slowly. "I could've sworn I put them in here." She started digging more frantically, then glanced at the cushions and the floor. "You've got to be kidding me."

"Alright, let's retrace your steps," Jayy said, standing and scanning the area. "You had them when you came in, right?"

"Obviously," she said, already on her feet.

They checked the couch, the bar counter, even the bathroom she'd ducked into earlier. Nothing.

"Lost keys at the end of the night? Rookie move," Jayy joked, trying to lighten the mood.

Before Luna could reply, a smooth voice cut through the quiet.

"Looking for something?" Myra's tone was calm, almost casual, but it carried an undercurrent that made Luna glance up despite herself.

"My keys," Luna replied curtly, not breaking her scan of the floor. "If you see them, let me know."

Jayy straightened, sensing the shift, his gaze flicking between them.

"You don't need to worry about it, Jayy," Myra said, lips curving into a faint smile. "I've got it. I'll help her find them." "You sure?" Jayy asked, hesitating.

"Positive," Myra replied firmly, her eyes never leaving Luna.

"Thanks for coming tonight. You've been great."

Jayy gave Luna a playful pat on the shoulder. "Good luck, superstar," he said with a smirk before heading toward the door.

The door swung shut, the latch clicking into place. Voices from the last staffers drifted down the hall, then faded. A key turned. The house seemed to exhale until only the low thrum of the playlist remained.

Luna exhaled slowly, frustration seeping into her words. "This isn't funny, Myra."

"Funny?" Myra's reply was light, almost airy. "I'm just trying to help."

The now empty house seemed to amplify every small sound, the click of Myra's heel against the floor, the faint rustle of Luna's jacket as she shifted. Myra tilted her head, taking a deliberate step closer. A glint of metal flashed between her fingers before disappearing back into her palm.

"Myra," Luna said, her voice low, warning threading through it.

"Give me my damn keys."

"Why are you in such a hurry to leave?" Myra asked softly, her tone steady but weighted with emotion. "You've been avoiding me for weeks, dodging every attempt I've made to talk to you. Now that I finally have you here, I'm not wasting the chance."

Luna's jaw tightened, her arms folding in a defensive cross. "This isn't the way to get me to stay," she said, firmer this time.

Myra's brow arched. "Then what is? You've been shutting me out, I've tried everything else."

"You mean like letting me walk in here tonight and see you with Jordan?" Luna's tone was sharp, the name dropping like a stone between them.

Myra's eyes narrowed, the faintest flicker of annoyance breaking through her composure. "That wasn't what it looked like."

Luna scoffed. "It looked exactly like it always does, chaos following you around while you claim you're trying to fix things."

"It was nothing," Myra said, her voice low but steady. "Jordan showed up uninvited. We exchanged words, that's it. You were the one I was looking for all night."

"Don't put that on me," Luna shot back, her jaw tight. "I'm still pissed about the last time we spoke. You can't just walk back into my life when it's convenient for you."

Myra took a slow step forward, closing the distance inch by inch. "This isn't about convenience. This is about not letting you walk out of here without knowing where I stand."

Luna opened her mouth to respond, but the words caught when Myra's hands came to rest lightly on her hips. The touch was gentle, unassuming, yet it sent an unwelcome ripple of heat through her chest.

"What are you doing?" Luna asked, her voice strained, though she didn't step away.

Myra's gaze softened, vulnerability peeking through the confident mask she so carefully wore. She leaned in, her breath brushing Luna's cheek.

"Don't think you can fix years of pain with a kiss," Luna said sharply, her voice trembling despite the steel in her words.

"Something I should've done a long time ago," Myra murmured.

"Myra, don't—" But her protest was cut off as Myra's lips met hers, tentative yet unyielding. Luna stiffened, every muscle fighting the pull, but as Myra's hands slid to the small of her back, anchoring her in place, her resistance faltered. Against her better judgment, she found herself giving in.

Myra's lips brushed hers again, softer this time, like a question instead of a demand. Luna froze, her breath hitching despite herself. The taste of champagne still lingered between them, mingling with something far more dangerous: hope.

Her hands came up, palms pressing against Myra's chest—not to shove her away, but to hold her there, suspended in that maddeningly fragile moment.

"Myra…" Luna's voice cracked around her name, equal parts warning and plea.

Myra searched her eyes, the flicker of vulnerability still there, raw and unguarded. "I'm not asking you to forget. I'm asking you to remember why we ever mattered in the first place."

Luna's heart thudded in her chest, too loud in the hush of the nearly empty room. Every instinct told her to turn, to leave before she let Myra dismantle the walls she'd fought so hard to build. But her body betrayed her, leaning in ever so slightly, caught between the gravity of old wounds and the pull of something she still wanted more than she cared to admit.

"It's not that simple," Luna shot back, her eyes narrowing. "You can't erase what happened just because you've decided you want me again."

Myra's gaze didn't waver. "Want you again? Luna, I never stopped."

That one line lodged in Luna's chest, cutting past the anger she'd been clinging to. Her jaw tightened, but her voice softened without her permission. "Then why does it feel like you only fight for me when you're about to lose me?"

Myra stepped in, closing the space between them. "Because I'm scared as hell of losing you for good."

The admission landed heavy in the air between them. Luna's pulse spiked, her resolve slipping as Myra's eyes held hers.

Without another word, Myra leaned in, and their lips met again—slow, deliberate, tasting of all the things left unsaid. They both held on to that kiss until there was a need for oxygen.

Both released at the same time, coming up for air, and their lips met with another passionate kiss. Myra eased back a breath, slid a hand into her pocket, and pressed the cool ring of keys into Luna's palm, closing her fingers around it.

"Yours," she whispered. "You say when."

A beat. The metal warmed in Luna's hand. She tucked the keys into her blazer, eyes never leaving Myra's. "Stay," she said, voice steady. "I want this." "Okay."

Myra's answer was a nod, a promise, then her mouth found

Luna's again.

This time, Luna ran her hands down Myra's side, gripped her hips, and pulled her closer, thinking to herself: *finally, I have you.*

It was driving Myra crazy being this close to Luna. God, she smelled so good, and her lips were just as soft as she had dreamed they would be for so long.

Luna granted Myra access to deepen the kiss, their tongues meeting for the first time. Myra moaned into her mouth as they fought for dominance, the air between them charged and hungry.

Myra broke from her lips just long enough to breathe, her mouth finding the curve of Luna's neck. Luna gasped in approval at the first feel of Myra's lips on her skin. She gripped Myra's hips tighter, pressing their bodies together, their shared warmth drawing a low moan from both.

"I need you," Myra confessed before stealing another kiss.

Sliding one leg between Luna's, Myra brushed her thigh against her center.

"Then take me," Luna breathed.

The dominance in her words lit something in Myra. She trailed wet kisses along Luna's neck, licking and leaving love bites, her hand traveling up Luna's sides until it slipped under her top. With a flick of her fingers, she unhooked her bra in one smooth motion, smirking to herself.

The feel of Myra's fingers teasing her nipples sent a shiver straight to Luna's core. Myra stepped back just enough to pull her shirt and lacy black bra over her head, dropping them to the floor.

Her mouth closed around a hardened nipple, teeth grazing before her tongue swirled in slow, deliberate circles. Luna's moan echoed through the room, rich and unrestrained. She pulled Myra back up, capturing her lips before tugging off her shirt and bra in return.

Myra paused, catching her breath as she met Luna's lust-filled gaze. Luna smirked before lowering her mouth to Myra's breasts, tracing wet circles around her nipples, alternating between gentle sucks and teasing flicks of her tongue.

She released Myra's breasts and began trailing open-mouthed kisses down the center of her stomach, her touch leaving Myra's muscles twitching with anticipation. Her hands gripped Myra's ass firmly before gliding over her hips, fingers finding the edge of her panties and tugging them down.

Her fingertips explored the soft skin of Myra's thighs, spreading them wider before lowering her mouth. Luna's tongue swept through her folds, the flick against her clit pulling a sharp gasp from Myra's lips. She tried to hold back her moans, but the sensation made it impossible.

Luna slid her fingers through Myra's wetness, rubbing over her clit before pressing two fingers inside her, slow at first, then building a steady rhythm.

"I've missed you," Luna admitted between kisses to Myra's stomach, her voice low and raw. "I've been craving the way you taste… craving those sweet moans."

Her fingers curled just right, making Myra's hips rock into her hand.

"Fuck," Myra gasped, pressing her forehead against Luna's, her eyes squeezed shut. "That feels so fucking good."

Luna's moans vibrated against her as she kept her pace, her own body thrumming with need at the sight of Myra unraveling.

"Yes… that's it. So close, baby," she whispered, silently begging her to let go.

Her arm burned, but she didn't stop until Myra's breath caught, her body shaking as release ripped through her, clenching around Luna's fingers. Luna's eyes locked on her face, watching every second of her release before slowly pulling her fingers out. She brought them to her mouth, sucking them clean with a satisfied moan.

"You taste so good."

Myra smiled, pulling her into a deep kiss, moaning at the taste of herself on Luna's tongue.

She shifted, sliding down Luna's body until she was kneeling between her thighs. Her mouth closed around Luna's clit, sucking gently before flicking her tongue against it. Luna's hips jerked, her breath catching.

The tension in her stomach coiled tighter as Myra pressed two fingers inside her, matching the rhythm of her tongue. It only took moments before the pleasure broke, and she cried out, her toes curling as her body shook with release.

Myra crawled back up, leaving soft kisses along her skin until she reached her neck. Luna wrapped her arms around her, their breathing heavy in the quiet.

Myra rested her head against Luna's chest, listening to her heartbeat slow.

"Damn," was all Luna could manage when her breathing finally evened out.

Myra laughed into her skin. This was what she had wanted: finally feeling their bare skin against each other, no more distance. She pressed one last kiss to Luna's collarbone and curled into her softly.

CHAPTER 22
CHOOSING, NOT CHASING

Saturday Morning Light

Myra woke to a slice of pale sun on the wall and the cool dip in the mattress where Luna had been. The sheet still held a faint citrus-and-warm-skin scent; a glass of water sat on the nightstand, a lipstick crescent on the rim.

Her phone buzzed. A 6:07 a.m. text.

Luna: Locked your door. Early call at the studio. Thank you for last night.

Myra smiled into the pillow and stared at the ceiling until the smile hurt. Then the ache crept in, soft, uncertain.

Don't rush her, she told herself. *Don't rush this.*

She showered, tied her robe, poured coffee, and typed a message she didn't send: *Last night wasn't a moment to me. I want to build something real, with time, with care.* She let it sit in drafts like a bird on a windowsill, not ready to fly.

Across town, Luna sat in her car, both hands gripping the wheel as if the leather could steady her. The studio lights flickered awake inside. Her pulse hadn't quite decided if it was grateful or terrified.

She opened Myra's text draft in her mind—the one that didn't exist yet—and answered it with a breath she couldn't send: *Me too.* Then she pocketed it, went inside, and turned on the music for the morning set-up.

Monday – The Space Between

Luna's routine ran like it always did: treadmill, steam, black mug, inbox. The only glitch was the quiet place behind her ribs that kept replaying the way Myra had said her name in the dark.

Nikki leaned in the doorway, heel tapping to a silent metronome. "You do realize you're stirring air with that spoon and the coffee's already consumed, right?"

Luna looked down at the empty mug; the spoon still moving.

"I'm… pre-caffeinated."

"Uh-huh." Nikki crossed to the desk and set down the day's run. "Two consults, a test shoot, and the product call at three. Anything I should know about your brain before we walk into that?"

"It's fine."

"Fine like eyebrows-on-fleek fine, or fine like 'my heart is pacing in stilettos' fine?"

"Niks." Luna said with a stern look.

Nikki softened, dropping her voice. "You leaving at dawn after… whatever… does not make you a villain. Just… don't ghost the part of you that wants things."

Luna didn't answer. She didn't have to; the silence said she heard it.

That night, Myra stood at her dresser in a pinstripe suit, cufflinks catching the lamplight. She opened the drafts folder, reread the message, and finally hit send.

Myra: Last night wasn't a moment to me. I want to build something real with time, with care.

She set the phone down as if it might bite and practiced breathing slowly.

Tuesday Almost Reply

At lunch, Luna read the text three times in the studio break room, thumb hovering, chest tight. She typed Same, then deleted it. Typed *I'm scared*, then deleted that too. She chose nothing and put the phone face-down—not to punish, but to think.

Back in the main room, Nikki handed her a water and didn't comment on the way Luna's eyes kept flicking to the door every time it opened.

"You're allowed to want it and still take your time," Nikki murmured, like she'd read her mind.

"Taking my time," Luna said, making the words a small promise.

That evening, Myra worked late with a playlist on low—D'Angelo, Snoh, a little H.E.R.—and closed a small duplex like it would keep her hands busy and her head quiet. It didn't.

She reread the read receipt (none) and told herself: *Space isn't silence. Space is care.*

Wednesday — Clear to Close

At 10:14 a.m., Myra's phone lit up with the message she'd been waiting on from title.

Title: Clear to close.

She smiled—clean and real—and, without overthinking, forwarded it.

Myra: We've got the clear to close. Thought you'd want to know.

Thursday Night

On the other side of the city, Luna felt it land in her palm like a key. It wasn't just the house; it was proof they could move a thing from blueprint to finish line without burning it down.

She stared at the text for a long beat, then wrote back and erased three versions. She didn't send anything. Instead, she walked to the window, watched a cloud pull across the sun, and chose her next move with her feet, not her thumbs.

The warm spill of Myra's office lights cut a soft rectangle into the hallway. Luna hesitated at the threshold like the room had a pulse, then stepped in.

Myra looked up from her desk, a glass of sparkling water in her hand and that tired, real smile that always hit first and deepest. "You came."

"I said I would." Luna slipped her hands into her blazer pockets, like her nerves could hide there. "Congrats on clear to close."

Myra's mouth tilted. "Couldn't have done it without you."

Silence settled—the good kind, full instead of empty. The city glowed in the window behind Myra, a quilt of small, patient lights.

"I meant what I texted," Myra said, voice steady but soft. "that night wasn't just a moment for me. I don't want to rush us. I want to build… on purpose."

Luna nodded, jaw easing like a hand had finally unclenched it. "I don't have a speech. I have boundaries." A breath. "Slow. Honest. No pretending. And no disappearing—either of us."

Myra's shoulders dropped half an inch, the exact weight of relief. "Deal."

They let it hang there—the terms, the tenderness—without grabbing for more. Myra rounded the desk, stopping a step away, close enough to share the air, not so close it asked for anything else.

"I have the final walk-through first thing tomorrow," she said, a little grin sneaking in. "Nine a.m., before closing. Come with me."

A beat. Luna felt the answer arrive before she said it. "Yeah. I want to see it with you." Myra's eyes warmed. "Then it's a date." She caught herself, winced, laughed. "A… realtor-approved appointment."

"Mm." Luna pretended to consider. "Those are my favorite kind."

Myra leaned a shoulder to the glass, looking at her like the past didn't have to crowd the room anymore. "We don't have to solve everything tonight. We can just… show up tomorrow. Let the house talk."

"Okay," Luna said. "Tomorrow."

Myra reached for her hand, just a link, not a pull. Luna let their fingers lace and felt the small, electric truth of it: *choosing, not chasing.*

"I'll text you the gate code," Myra said. "I'll have the packet ready. Pens, tabs, the whole circus."

"And bread after," Luna countered. "Somewhere with bad lighting."

"I know exactly the place."

They didn't kiss. They didn't test the edges of what they had just agreed to. Myra squeezed once—*I see you*—and let go first, the gentlest proof that she meant what she had said about pace.

At the door, Luna paused, palm on the frame. "For what it's worth… I didn't leave because I regretted it. I left so I wouldn't ask a brand-new thing to carry everything we haven't said yet."

Myra's answer was a quiet, grateful exhale. "Thank you for saying that."

"Text me the code," Luna said. "You'll actually answer?" Myra teased. "Hold me to it."

"I will."

Luna stepped into the hallway, the night cool against her face. Behind her, Myra's lamp clicked off. Ahead of her, morning waited: keys, light, and a house that already knew their names.

CHAPTER 23
ON PURPOSE

Myra

She got there ten minutes early because she always did and unlocked the front door to let the morning in. The house answered with quiet: sunlight sliding over the hardwood, the soft tick of cooling ducts, that clean, faintly sweet smell of fresh paint and new wood.

She did a quick, efficient sweep lights, outlets, cabinet hinges blue tape tucked behind her ear like a pencil. Pens and the punch- list sat neat on the island, a stack of polished keys under a paperweight she would not move until it was official.

When her phone buzzed, she didn't have to look. "Gate code still the same?" "Yep. Door's open."

A minute later, tires hummed over the drive. Myra smoothed her blazer, told her pulse to relax, and stood just inside the foyer where the afternoon would someday throw light across the stairs.

The door eased wider. Luna

She paused on the threshold, letting the quiet spill over her like a warm cloth. Today the house didn't feel like a listing. It felt like a held breath.

"Hey," Myra said, and there was no rush in it.

"Hey," Luna answered, stepping in. Black suit. Gold hoops. Calm she wore like a tailored thing. Her eyes did a slow lap:

the line of the staircase, the lift of the ceiling, the way light gathered on the floor like water finding level.

"I'll give you space," Myra murmured. "Do your first pass. I'll be… floating." "Good," Luna said, grateful for the permission. "I need to hear it."

She slipped off her shoes, felt the cool of the floor through thin socks, and let her hand ride the banister as she climbed.

Luna – Upstairs

The second floor opened like a promise: hallway, clean and bright; the whisper of a vent; the faint, new-house hush that made her aware of her own breath.

She took the rooms in order: the office, with its square of perfect morning light on the wall where a canvas would live; the guest room, that felt instantly like a place people would tell long stories in; a linen closet, that smelled like cotton and sawdust and something uncomplicated.

Then the primary bedroom. She stopped in the doorway.

White walls. Light gray curtains pooled just so. The blue of the staging blanket wasn't the exact shade from her dream, but it was close enough to pull something at the center of her chest.

She crossed to the window and pressed her palm to the glass. The view was what she remembered: sky, line of trees, a sliver of city beyond. She tested the latch, the weight, the sound of it clicking home. She turned and stood where a bed would go. She imagined morning exactly here, the kind that begins with the quiet certainty of being known.

Can a house forgive you for wanting too much?

Can a house hold the artist, the boss, the girl who leaves before sunrise, and the woman who stays?

The room didn't answer; it didn't need to. It just offered itself: edges, light, air. Enough.

"Okay," she said to nobody, and felt the word settle.

Myra – Upstairs

She didn't follow at first. She did the professional things: ran the water until it turned hot, checked for drips under the sink, opened and closed the oven like she hadn't done it twice already. Every few minutes she caught herself listening for the whisper of steps above her.

Don't sell this to her heart. Let the house do it.

When she finally headed up, she took the back stair to give Luna more room to breathe. She paused in the hall, adjusting a crooked staging frame with two fingers, a habit more than a need. The master bedroom door was open. She could see only the foot of the bed, the soft fall of the gray curtains, a corner of blue.

She stayed in the hallway and did her own small inventory: baseboards clean, paint lines crisp, those extra outlets she had insisted on at the vanity for curling irons, camera lights, and a life built in layers. Little ways she had been thinking of this woman even when she was pretending she wasn't.

Footsteps shifted in the room. Myra looked up, and there Luna was, turned toward the window, one hand in her pocket like she was anchoring herself.

Myra didn't step in. She didn't have to.

They met at the landing, not quite touching, the distance between them measured in inches and everything unsaid.

"How's it talking?" Myra asked lightly.

Luna's mouth tilted. "It's loud in here for a quiet house."

Myra's laugh was soft. "Good loud or run-for-your-life loud?"

"Good," Luna said. A beat. "The kind that sounds like… showing up."

They walked together for the second pass, no longer giving each other space and also giving each other all of it.

In the bathroom, Luna turned the shower on, watched the steam curl up. "Water pressure's a yes."

"Tankless," Myra said. "You can sing in there for hours."

"Bold to assume I sing," Luna murmured, trying not to smile, then failing anyway.

In the smallest bedroom, Myra tapped a spot on the wall. "We added blocking so you can hang shelves without hunting studs."

"Of course you did." Luna's chest went warm in a way that had nothing to do with carpentry.

Back in the hall, they stood by the laundry closet, listening to the dryer drum make its polite, new spin.

"We're nitpicking," Myra said. "Which is how I know it fits."

"It fits," Luna echoed, surprised at how certain the words felt in her mouth.

They ended in the bedroom because that's where gravity put them. The light had shifted brighter now, a pale ribbon across the floorboards where their socks stood side by side.

"Feels like we dreamed this room before we found it," Luna said, almost to the window.

Myra's answer was simple: "We did."

She didn't move closer. She didn't push. She slipped the roll of blue tape from behind her ear and held it out.

"If there's anything you don't love, mark it," she said. "I want it right."

Luna took the tape, tore off a square, and stuck it next to the tiniest scuff near the baseboard. Another by a paint nib most people wouldn't notice. Myra watched the small care of it, the way claiming things looked on her.

"I'm nitpicking because it's mine," Luna said, then blinked at herself, surprised and not.

Myra's smile was quiet and complete. "Good."

They drifted back to the kitchen. The documents waited on the island, corners squared, pen centered. Myra slid the stack forward with practiced calm, though her fingers weren't as steady as usual.

"This is it," she said, tone steady. "Once you sign, the house is officially yours."

Luna picked up the pen, feeling its cool weight. She hesitated, eyes lifting to Myra's. "You know this isn't just about a house for me. It's more than that."

Myra's expression softened, something unguarded flickering beneath the professional poise. "I know," she said quietly. "It's a fresh start."

A small smile tugged at Luna's mouth. "And I have you to thank for it."

Myra's breath caught, barely, but she recovered, the faintest grin smoothing it over. "It's my job," she teased, though the thread of emotion in her voice gave her away.

Initial here. Sign there. Date. One last signature, and the pen clicked down with a soft finality that felt bigger than ink on paper.

Myra gathered the pages, careful and deliberate. When she looked up, their eyes met, and the air between them hummed.

"Congratulations," she said, warm and low. "You're officially a homeowner."

Relief, and something like wonder, moved through Luna.

"Thanks, Myra. For everything."

Myra reached into her tote and set a small ring of keys in Luna's palm. "Welcome home."

Luna stood at the threshold of the moment, the keys cool against her skin. It wasn't just square footage and fixtures. It was a stake in the ground, a life she was choosing on purpose.

She turned back. Myra lingered near the door, tailored and composed, yet somehow softer than all of that. Luna's voice came out steady, threaded with meaning. "This house… it's beautiful. It's everything I wanted. But it's just walls and floors without you."

Myra's smile rose slow and bright, lighting her whole face. "You have a way of making a girl feel special, you know that?"

"Only the ones who deserve it," Luna said, tugging her gently closer.

For a moment they stood in the entryway, letting the past exhale around them while the future took shape. Myra's thumb traced across Luna's knuckles. "So… where do we start?"

Luna tilted her head, eyes sparking. "How about with a toast? To us. To this house. To everything we're about to build."

"I'll drink to that," Myra whispered at her cheek.

Myra opened the fridge and pulled a chilled bottle from the back, already there, already waiting, along with two slim flutes.

"To us," Myra said, lifting her glass.

"To us," Luna echoed. Crystal touched crystal, sharp and bright, full of possibility.

They sipped, and the quiet wrapped around them like a welcome. No static. No old gravity. Just the soft thrum of a home taking them in.

Luna set her glass down, met Myra's eyes, and didn't look away. "Stay tonight," she said. Then, softer, braver: "Stay forever."

Myra's smile widened, a yes blooming across her whole face. "I was hoping you'd ask."

They closed the space between them. The kiss was gentle and certain, promise over heat. No rush. No running. Just two women stepping into a life they had both imagined, now finally, on purpose.

ACKNOWLEDGMENTS

I wrote this book because I needed to heal. When there is no real closure, the words become the only place where the fragments of you story can finally rest. This book was born from pieces of me I wasn't sure I'd ever share — the broken parts, the vulnerable parts, the parts that once felt like they had no voice.

Writing these pages became my way of finding light when everything felt heavy, and of discovering that even pain can be transformed into something meaningful. To those who stood beside me while I stumbled through the dark —Thank you. To the friends who reminded me I wasn't alone, to the ones who offered listening ears when I had no more words left, and to those who gave me space to be quiet when silence was the only thing I could manage — you carried me when I couldn't carry myself. Your love became the anchor that held me steady when grief tried to pull me under.

To the people who hurt me and left me without answers — you unknowingly gave me the material that built these chapters. You taught me that closure isn't always something another person can give; Sometimes it's something you must create for yourself. This book is my closure. It is me choosing myself, my voice, and my healing. And finally, to every reader holding this book in your hands — this story no longer belongs only to me. If you've ever searched for closure, if you've ever tried to put yourself back together after being undone, I hope these pages remind you that healing is possible, even when it feels unreachable. This book is as much yours as it is mine.

ABOUT THE AUTHOR

B. D. Sinclair is a storyteller, creative, and lifelong lover of words. With a passion for exploring love, loss, and self-discovery, she writes stories that speak to the heart. When she isn't writing, she's dreaming up new ideas, sipping on coffee, or enjoying quiet moments by the water.

Five Years Too Long
is her debut novel.